Leprechauns

The Myths, Legends, & Lore

Bob Curran

Adams Media

New York London Toronto Sydney New Delhi

Adams media

Adams Media
An Imprint of Simon & Schuster, Inc.
57 Littlefield Street
Avon, Massachusetts 02322

Copyright © 2019 by Bob Curran.

All rights reserved, including the right to reproduce this book or portions thereof in any form whatsoever. For information address Adams Media Subsidiary Rights Department, 1230 Avenue of the Americas, New York, NY 10020.

First Adams Media hardcover edition February 2019

ADAMS MEDIA and colophon are trademarks of Simon & Schuster.

For information about special discounts for bulk purchases, please contact Simon & Schuster Special Sales at 1-866-506-1949 or business@simonandschuster.com.

The Simon & Schuster Speakers Bureau can bring authors to your live event. For more information or to book an event contact the Simon & Schuster Speakers Bureau at 1-866-248-3049 or visit our website at www.simonspeakers.com.

Interior design by Katrina Machado
Interior images © Getty Images/ANGELGILD, geraria, olenadesign, MarinaMariya, maodesign, Druzhinina, Nastasic, whitemay, Pimonova, MorePics, Morphart, la_puma, Grafissimo, mrtom-uk, MarinaVorontsova, DenPotisev, Pimonova, neildev, song_mi, clu, ZU_09, duncan1890, VeraPetruk, Stymie924, seamartini, Maksym Zakhariuk, eyewave, SongSpeckels, los_ojos_pardos; Clipart.com; Wikimedia Commons/W.H. Brooke, FrancisTyers~commonswiki, Bob Burkhardt, T.C. Croker

Manufactured in the United States of America

10 9 8 7 6 5 4 3 2 1

Library of Congress Cataloging-in-Publication Data
Names: Curran, Bob, author.
Title: Leprechauns / Bob Curran.
Description: Avon, Massachusetts: Adams Media, 2019.
Includes index.
Identifiers: LCCN 2018024003 (print) | LCCN 2018031095 (ebook) | ISBN 9781507208922 (hc) | ISBN 9781507208939 (ebook)
Subjects: LCSH: Leprechauns. | Folklore--Ireland.
Classification: LCC GR153.5 (ebook) | LCC GR153.5 .C7694 2019 (print) | DDC 398.209417--dc23
LC record available at https://lccn.loc.gov/2018024003

ISBN 978-1-5072-0892-2
ISBN 978-1-5072-0893-9 (ebook)

Many of the designations used by manufacturers and sellers to distinguish their products are claimed as trademarks. Where those designations appear in this book and Simon & Schuster, Inc., was aware of a trademark claim, the designations have been printed with initial capital letters.

Adapted from *The Truth about Leprechauns* published by The O'Brien Press Ltd (2017). Originally published as *The Truth about the Leprechaun* by Wolfhound Press (2000). Text copyright © 2000, 2019 by Bob Curran.

Typesetting, layout, design, and editing copyright © 2019 by Adams Media, an Imprint of Simon & Schuster, Inc.

CONTENTS

INTRODUCTION 5

PART I: Who Are the Little People? 7

    Chapter 1: The Origins of
    Leprechauns 9

    Chapter 2: What Do
    Leprechauns Look Like? 23

    Chapter 3: Where to Find Leprechauns 31

    Chapter 4: What Do They Eat
    and Drink? 47

    Chapter 5: Are There Female
    Leprechauns? 55

    Chapter 6: How Long Do
    Leprechauns Live? 79

PART II: What Do Leprechauns Do? 87

    Chapter 7: Shoemakers, Builders,
    and Blacksmiths 89

    Chapter 8: Musicians, Music,
    and Festivals 97

    Chapter 9: Leprechaun Entertainment 111

    Chapter 10: Guardians of Gold 117

PART III: How Do Leprechauns Live? 127

    Chapter 11: Leprechaun Society 129

    Chapter 12: Leprechaun Law 141

    Chapter 13: Leprechauns and
    Religion 147

    Chapter 14: Leprechauns and
    the Dead 161

    Chapter 15: Other Wee Creatures 169

    Chapter 16: The Cluricaun
    and Others 183

    Chapter 17: Leprechauns in
    Popular Culture 193

CONCLUSION 215

INDEX 217

INTRODUCTION

Up the airy mountain,
Down the rushy glen,
We daren't go a-hunting,
For fear of little men.

—William Allingham, "The Fairies"

Who doesn't love a leprechaun? Clad in green, with tall hats and puffing on curved pipes, they are inseparable from Ireland. They're cheerful but elusive—if you're lucky enough to catch one, he may reveal to you his pot of gold, but beware! He's tricky and clever.

That's the popular image of these legendary creatures. But they have a darker, more sinister side. They're willing and able to take revenge on any they think have wronged them, and often their mischief is malicious and harmful. Leprechauns on the whole are extremely spiteful; they are as likely to perform an evil trick on the unwary mortal as a helpful or kindly one.

In this book, we'll explore the world of the leprechaun. We'll meet many humans who have come into contact with these strange beings and have either gained or lost from the encounter. And we'll learn some of the dark truths behind the fairy stories.

Leprechauns are fairies who belong to the Otherworld—an ill-defined realm that exists just beyond mortal sight. They coexist with humankind throughout the rural countryside, but generally remain invisible to human eyes. Collectively, they are referred to as the Sídhe (meaning "dwellers of the mounds"—the word *sí* or *sídh* originally meant "a mound") or Tuatha dé Danann (meaning "followers of Danu," a goddess); but through the years, they became known in country folktales simply as "the little people."

As to the origins of Irish fairy beings, stories are many and varied. Some people believe at one time they were as tall as any human. In those days they were gods, but as people stopped worshiping them, they shrank to their present size. Others say that they are angels who refused to take sides in the great conflict between God and Lucifer. For this, they were not wicked enough to fall into Hell but not good enough to sit in Heaven.

Whatever the truth of the matter, Irish—particularly those living in the countryside—have learned that leprechauns must be taken seriously. Now let's begin our journey to discover more about this strange, magical race of beings.

PART I

WHO ARE THE LITTLE PEOPLE?

CHAPTER 1

THE ORIGINS OF LEPRECHAUNS

The leprechaun's origins in folklore are complex. As a character, he is a walking contradiction—he is stupid but at the same time crafty and scheming; he is kind and will work for nothing, but at the same time he is grasping and greedy; he is helpful, but at the same time surly and dismissive. How can all these attributes be reconciled?

The answer is that the leprechaun's origins may lie in a multiplicity of folk beliefs. He may have started out as a vague and ill-defined folk memory of some diminutive race that once coexisted with the early Celts. The leprechaun's origins may lie partly in Scotland. But they may also lie elsewhere in the Celtic world. In Brittany, for instance, there is still a strong belief in *fées*—tiny creatures who dwell in rocks and gullies.

These creatures try to avoid humans as much as they can; however, once again, they are not above playing tricks on or acting maliciously toward humans when their fancy takes them. It may well be that stories about them also influenced Irish folktales, as well as the imagery of the leprechaun. These memories may have mingled with the folk beliefs of other peoples, which also contained legends of small races and solitary dwarves, to create a kind of fairy stereotype that found its way into the general corpus of Irish folklore. These, of course, are only speculations, for any definitive answer concerning the origins of the leprechaun are lost in the mists of time and myth.

The Fairies

Leprechauns inhabit the misty world of the fairy people. Fairies were believed to be a very diverse species. Some lived in the air, some on the land, others in the sea, and others still under the earth—and each kind acquired some of the characteristics of their environment.

- The fairies of the air were light, graceful, and rather nebulous beings, often described as flitting about on gossamer-like wings.
- Fairies who lived in the sea were sometimes covered in fur, like the seals they clearly resembled, or in scales, like fish.
- Fairies who lived on the earth were invisible beings that dwelt in the raths and earthen forts that littered the countryside. They were tall and splendid beings—very like humans, it was said, but with an unearthly beauty about them.
- The fairies that lived under the earth—in mounds and caverns, in ditches and under hedgerows—were small, stunted beings with hard skins and even harder looks. They were often described as being "as brown as the earth" because of their harsh environment.

There is no way to determine an actual source, but it may be that they came from Europe, with waves of invaders who gradually settled in Ireland. Right across the Continent, we find tales of small, elusive aboriginal races dwelling in communities well away from their taller counterparts. Some of these little people were considered to have special powers; many are said to have lived underground, and many were believed to be ugly or slightly deformed (or different from humankind) in some way. Might these have been the prehistoric prototypes for the leprechaun?

ADAPTATIONS BY THE IRISH

The Irish leprechaun may be part of a much wider lore concerning small races and creatures. This lore includes brownies, gnomes, goblins, *fées*, and pixies, all of whom feature prominently in Celtic vernacular mythology. It is quite possible that many of the tales concerning leprechauns were adapted by the Irish from other sources, perhaps from outside their own shores. Since there is no reference to the *luchorpán* in Ireland before the seventh or eighth century, there seems little doubt that he was imported from elsewhere and was integrated into native mythologies.

A clue to the origins of the *luchorpán* comes from Ulster. Here, the leprechaun is known by two quite specific names—*grogoch* and *pecht*. It is the latter epithet, "pecht," that hints at the origin, for it is too close to the word *pict*—a generic name in the area for aboriginal Scottish peoples—to be simply coincidence. Old local people, particularly in the North Antrim area, are quite sure of the area from which their diminutive neighbors came to Ireland.

The Word *Leprechaun*

Despite its now-widespread appeal—it is used to refer to almost any Irish fairy—the term *leprechaun* was not really used until the late seventeenth or early eighteenth century. Even then, the word had many different, localized variations. In east Leinster, for example, the term was *liomreachán*, while in south Leinster it was *lúracán;* in Ulster it was *luchramán*, in Connacht *lúracán*. Even within provinces, the name varied. For instance, in parts of Munster, the sprite was called a *luchargán, lurgadán*, or *cluricáun*, while in other areas the description *luchorpán* prevailed.

Many of these descriptions were taken from the sprite's alleged powers or characteristics. Within these terms, there are echoes of the ancient Irish words *luch* ("mouse"), *lúth* ("agility"), and *lurga* ("ankle"). The leprechaun was, therefore, believed to be about the size of a mouse, with speedy reflexes and large feet. The term *leprechaun* is thought to have been used only in the north Leinster area until the middle or end of the nineteenth century. Nowadays, this form seems to be widely used all over Ireland.

THE BROWNIE

One creature who resembled leprechauns in some respects was the Scottish brownie. He was small, with large pointed ears and big eyes. After the household was asleep, he ventured out and helped with everyday chores, but he expected a reward in the form of food and drink. Readers of J.K. Rowling's Harry Potter series will recognize immediately the similarities to Dobby, the heroic house elf.

The origin of the term *leprechaun* is complex. It has been argued that it derives from *leith bhrógán* ("half-shoe–maker—maker of half a pair of shoes"), making the sprite a cobbler by profession, with a collection of related folklore attached to him. However, it is more likely that the name comes from the ancient Irish *luchorpán* ("little man") or *luacharmán* ("pygmy"), simply denoting a creature of very small stature. In texts dating from the eighth century, the term is used to denote members of a little race. In the legend of Fearghus mac Léide, for example, reference is made to a community of small people with magical powers and skills. Fearghus seizes three of them, and, in return for their release, they bestow the magical skills of swimming upon him. Later texts, dating from the tenth, eleventh, and twelfth centuries, say that these beings may also bestow certain magical objects, such as silver shoes that enable a person to walk on water without drowning.

Fairy Temperament

As well as taking on the physical characteristics of their environment, many fairies also acquired a temperamental quality that reflected their surroundings. Fairies of the air were shallow, fickle creatures, who changed their minds as often as the wind changed; the moods of water-fairies fluctuated with the tides; and those who dwelt under the earth and in remote places were usually surly and reclusive in their ways. Many were extremely hostile toward humans, and went out of their way to do mischief and inflict harm upon unwary mortals. In this respect, leprechauns are no different from other fairy folk.

In the late eighteenth and early nineteenth centuries, a more sophisticated folklore began to divide the fairy realm into two distinct camps. One camp consisted of the trooping fairies—what the poet W.B. Yeats called the Macara Shee, the fairy cavalcade: a band of supernatural beings, usually of diminutive size, who traveled the country roads on certain nights of the year, such as Halloween and May Eve. At such times, according to rural folklore, the doors of the fairy hills and mounds swung open and the troop came out, led by a king and queen. Depending upon whom they met upon the road, they responded with gifts or with disdain, sometimes rewarding kindness, at other times punishing evil deeds. However, warned the wise people of the countryside, it was as well to avoid them whenever possible and to keep off the moonlit roads as soon as the sun went down.

Solitary Fairies

The other half of fairydom was what Yeats and others referred to as "the solitary fairies": those supernatural beings who lived well away from humans and from other fairies and had very little to do with them. These beings dwelt in caves, holes, bogs, and ditches and remained invisible for most of the time. Mortals could sense their presence only when the fairies lured them into some danger (possibly resulting in death) or when the fairies were accidentally heard by some passerby. Among these solitary creatures were such entities as the banshee (a "woman of the fairies" who cried for those who were about to die), the *lianhan shee* (the fairy lover who lured men to their doom), the *dullahan* (a terrible headless figure who galloped through the night bringing doom, misery, and destruction to the houses that he passed), and the leprechaun (the fairy shoemaker).

While the banshee has passed, more or less, into ghostlore, and beings such as the dullahan and the lianhan shee have been all but forgotten, the leprechaun has acquired a status that has put him at the forefront of Irish fairy tales and folktales.

The Fairy of Ireland

Despite his solitary nature, the leprechaun appears to have been seen frequently in many parts of Ireland. Indeed, the leprechaun has become something of a symbol of Ireland itself (one might be tempted to say he is the "national elf"). He appears on tea towels, on linen, in porcelain ornaments, and on illustrated plates from the Emerald Isle. He has appeared in both films and cartoons as the only fairy sprite in Ireland.

This does both the leprechaun and the fairy world a disservice, for the creature also appears in neighboring parts of the world—in Scotland, in the Western Isles and in the North of England—and he forms part of a wide range of magical beings.

Most of the painted representations of the leprechaun show him to be a jolly, amiable, and carefree creature. He is the sort of sprite with whom one would like to share a winter's night beside a roaring fire, listening to his old, humorous tales and sharing his poteen. He is the epitome of Irish hospitality and Irish storytelling.

The leprechaun is anything but amiable and humorous. He is dark and somber, with little or no levity about him. Nor is he particularly good company, for he seems to carry the woes of the world with him. Leprechauns are also great misers and extremely selfish, so there is little chance of them sharing anything, let alone their stores of poteen. Not only this, but leprechauns on the whole are extremely spiteful; they are as likely to perform an evil trick on the unwary mortal as a helpful or kindly one.

> ## POTEEN
> Poteen, or poitín, (pronounced "PUTT-cheen") is a distilled Irish drink that can be made from grain, sugar beets, molasses, or potatoes. It was usually manufactured illegally.

Because of their uncivil nature and innate hostility toward humans, leprechauns frequently had to be placated by the householders of the area. Failure to do so would invite mischief upon both family and property. Offerings of milk, cheese, bread, and other foodstuffs, as well as twists of tobacco, were sometimes left outside cottage doors at night, to keep the leprechaun from making mischief against the owner or tenant of the dwelling. Fresh water, the dregs of the teapot, or a glass of strong liquor were often left out as well. Sometimes libations of whiskey were left on the doorstep, but this alcoholic gift could have an adverse effect upon the sprite.

"Never leave too much whiskey for the leprechaun," conventional rural wisdom states, "for if you do, he'll only get very drunk and create a commotion around your house." It is also said that the whiskey may addle his wits and make him even more malignant than he already is.

Leprechauns have to be treated carefully, even when one is offering them presents.

> ### PURSE OF THE SHILLING
> In some parts of Munster, once in a while, a more amiable leprechaun will sometimes present an individual with a *sparán na scillinge* ("purse of the shilling")—a marvelous pouch that never becomes empty. However, although it is a wonderful present, there is a malicious reason for this particular gift. Those to whom it is given invariably misuse it—usually becoming drunkards and gamblers—and eventually all their wealth turns to dust and ashes. The leprechaun's present turns out to be a double-edged sword.

Signs of a Leprechaun

Ancient tradition said that the Tuatha dé Danann were usually invisible beings who existed, unseen by mortals, among the raths and forts of the countryside. The same is true of the leprechaun, who went about his business beyond the human gaze. The only sign of his presence was, perhaps, a small whirlwind or cloud of dust. In former times (and, in some areas, up until the present day), old men would doff their hats and old ladies would drop a small curtsy as one of these small dust storms swept past. In some areas, it was also common to bend a knee and say, "God bless me" or to throw your left shoe after the cloud; if you did, the leprechaun would be compelled to drop whatever he was carrying—which, if fortune was smiling, might be a bag of gold.

Abducting Humans

These pillars of dust might also be a sign that the leprechauns were carrying some unfortunate human off to the fairy realm. Leprechauns seem to have had a fondness for abducting unbaptized human babies, whom they then sold into service in the various forts (raths) and mounds. To protect children from such wiles, it was necessary to have an infant baptized by a clergyman as quickly as possible. In some more remote areas, where clerics were not readily available, the midwife who delivered the infant could perform an interim baptism using the following formula:

> No seed of fairy, no seed of the hosts of the air, no seed of the world's people can lift away this tranquil little sleeper for whom is made this beneficent prayer of baptism. Evil cannot lie on him [sign of the cross]; envy cannot lie on him [sign of the cross]; malice cannot lie on him [sign of the cross]. The two arms of mild Mary, the Mother of God, graciously encompass him; the two arms of the gentle Christ shield, surround and succour this joyous little sleeper of the baptism.

This particular baptism was used by midwives as far away as the Outer Hebrides of the coast of Scotland to protect newborn infants from the *taran*—a specific type of leprechaun-like creature. Two sim-

CHAPTER 1: THE ORIGINS OF LEPRECHAUNS

ilar non-clerical protective baptisms reputedly come from the west of Ireland, although they are also found in various parts of Scotland:

> When the image of the God of Life is brought into the world, I put three little drops of water on the child's forehead. I put the first little drop in the name of the Father (and the watching women say "Amen"); I put the second little drop in the name of the Son (and the watching women say "Amen"); I put the third little drop in the name of the Spirit (and the watching women say "Amen"). And I beseech the Holy Three to lave and to bathe the child and to preserve it to Themselves, protecting it from any evil thing—witch, goblin, or evil spirit. Let no dark thing come near to it or disturb its rest (and the watching women say "Amen").

PART I: WHO ARE THE LITTLE PEOPLE?

The second baptism uses roughly similar language and imagery:

> The little drop of the Father
> On thy little forehead, beloved one.
> The little drop of the Son
> On thy little forehead, beloved one.
> The little drop of the Spirit
> On thy little forehead, beloved one.
> To aid thee from the fays,
> To guard thee from the host,
> To aid thee from the gnome,
> To shield thee from the specter.
> To keep thee for the Three,
> To shield thee, to surround thee.
> To save thee for the Three,
> To fill thee with the graces.
> The little drop of the Three,
> To lave thee with the graces.

If any of the baptisms were performed by the midwife, then the crafty leprechauns (or any other fairy or witch, for that matter) had no power over the child. Of course, a full clerical baptism had to be performed as soon as possible, but the incantations had the power to restrain all members of the fairy kind until this could be achieved.

If neither a cleric nor a midwife were present at the birth, all the father of the child had to do was throw his coat or an item of his clothing over the sleeping infant. This, presumably, was to remind the fairy world that the child had been claimed by the human world, until a cleric could arrive.

Even then, it was believed that children still might not be safe from the leprechauns. Small children were strongly advised not to address a leprechaun directly or to give direct answers to any questions the creature might ask, since doing so would place the mortal in the fairy's power; he or she could be whisked off in a magic wind, to be sold in a fairy market or at the door of some rath or mound.

Far from being the jolly little fellow who appears on postcards and ornaments from Ireland, then, the leprechaun is a surly, miserly, mischievous, and antisocial being. Rather than being sought out by mortals, he was more likely to be feared.

Nevertheless, he played a central role in the fairy world, and he deserves to be studied in a bit more depth.

THE TUATHA DÉ DANANN

The Tuatha dé Danann were a very ancient people in Ireland, deities of Irish mythology. Each of them represents a particular power. On the whole, they were benevolent. Their origins lay in four cities in the north of Ireland (Falias, Gorias, Murias, and Finias) and they first made their appearance in Connaught.

CHAPTER 2

WHAT DO LEPRECHAUNS LOOK LIKE?

Although the image of the "wee man" on Irish or Irish-related products is fairly consistent—a jolly little fellow all dressed in green (to symbolize the greenness and lushness of Ireland)—folkloric accounts of the leprechaun vary greatly.

The first problem is that of size. Some tales describe him as extremely small—"a wee man, no bigger than a thumbnail," small enough to hold in the palm of one's hand. Other stories describe him as being about the size of a two-year-old child, which places him in an almost-human category. The size of the sprite frequently depends upon where he is seen. If he is glimpsed hidden under hedges or in *sheughs* ("gullies") or ditches, then he tends to be much smaller, in order to increase his powers of concealment. If he lives in a cave, on the other hand, or in a ruined building, he may be slightly larger, since concealment is not absolutely necessary.

Whatever his size, however, all accounts agree that the leprechaun is usually an untidy and disheveled being. His clothing, reflecting the rather haphazard dress of the nineteenth-century Irish peasantry, is not at all stylish. There is none of the coordination of freshly laundered green clothes that appears in stereotyped pictures of him. Instead, he will probably wear an old green (or bottle-blue) dress coat, red breeches buckled at the knee, thick woolen stockings, and a wide-brimmed hat, generally slightly askew. Sometimes he will wear a "claw-hammer" coat (an old type of formal dress coat, which sports a forked tail, typically worn by what was once known as the "down-at-heel gentry"). If he wears a shirt, it will be dirty and worn, tucked untidily into his broad belt, giving him an unkempt appearance. The overall impression made by his clothing is either that of the "reduced Catholic former aristocracy" during the late eighteenth and early nineteenth centuries, when leprechaun mythology began to develop in Ireland, or that of the itinerant working classes that spread throughout the countryside during the same period—"not rich enough to be comfortable, nor poor enough to be destitute."

Keeping Warm and Comfortable

Occasionally, the leprechaun will wear a red stocking cap like a nineteenth-century mariner's. This is simply a piece of red material, drawn into a shape very much like a nightcap and crudely stitched together. Invariably, the stitching is very untidy, as the leprechaun has no skill with a needle and thread. The cap is then pulled well down over the ears for added warmth. Some leprechauns will wear an old tricorn hat, set at a jaunty angle. This gives them a slightly "roguish" air and makes them (they believe) more attractive to human women.

> ## LEPRECON
>
> Leprechauns as such do not feature in the Artemis Fowl novels written by Eoin Colfer. Nonetheless, they make an appearance— sort of. The novels are about Artemis Fowl, a twelve-year-old criminal genius. In the first book of the series, he kidnaps and holds for ransom a fairy. The Lower Elements Police send one of their best officers, Holly Short, to retrieve the fairy from Fowl. Short is a captain of a reconnaissance division of the LEP. Hence the name: LEPrecon.
>
> Curiously, Short and Fowl become close friends and join forces in other books to prevent various worldwide disasters.

Given that leprechauns often live in damp, cold places, personal insulation is extremely important to them. Consequently, many wear several layers of clothing, as a protection against the chill of their dank habitats. Despite being encumbered with so much clothing, the sprite is still extremely agile and fleet of foot, and the fact that he is wearing several rather heavy coats does not appear to slow him down when he is being pursued by mortals.

Footwear

Although shoes are reputedly the leprechaun's stock-in-trade and he is widely regarded (by humans) as the cobbler of the fairy world, his own footwear leaves a great deal to be desired. His shoes are usually badly worn and shabby, scuffed and muddied from long hours of crouching in gullies and drains.

The boots are made of a more flexible leather and are ornamented with silver buckles like an eighteenth-century dandy's. Many of these shoes also have slightly exaggerated heels built into them. This is to give the impression of height, because—although they very rarely mention it—leprechauns are extremely sensitive about their height.

Favored Colors

Greens and browns are the colors most favored by leprechauns—although the green is not the sharp Lincoln hue that appears in many artistic representations. These colors are favored for two reasons. First, they are the colors of concealment. To avoid capture by inquisitive mortals, the leprechaun has to dart through bushes and along muddy tracks, and these hues act as camouflage as he does so. He can therefore pass unseen by mortal eyes. Second, the brown shade matches the color of the sprite's skin, which is dusky and weather-beaten from so many hours in the open air and sun. All these colors seem to merge to give a kind of invisibility to the sprite as he moves through the undergrowth around his home.

The tints of the clothing are created using homemade dyes. The green and red dyes are extracted from lichens, which the leprechaun usually finds growing near his home, but he is also adept at using many other materials as they come to hand. This gives his clothing a kind of rough-and-ready appearance, and—especially as some leprechauns appear to vary in size at certain times of the year, thus making their clothing seem ill-fitting—it adds to his overall air of dishevelment.

> **IRON BOOTS**
>
> According to some traditions, in olden days leprechauns wore iron boots for durability; but as humans began to spread across the country, leprechauns were forced to abandon these, since the clanking and scraping of the metal frequently drew attention to their movements. The boots must also have been extremely heavy and uncomfortable to wear.

Cleanliness—or Not

Because leprechauns have a natural aversion to water, few of them wash with any sort of regularity. Furthermore, due to the heavy layers of clothing some of them wear, they tend to be extremely sweaty, especially in summer. Not being the most hygienic of creatures, they allow the sweat to dry on their skins, thus creating a personal stench that would make many of the strongest mortals flinch.

This personal odor is greatly exacerbated by the fact that many leprechauns smoke dudeens, foul-smelling clay pipes. Though he very rarely smokes tobacco, the leprechaun usually finds enough leaves and other items to give off a pungent reek. According to one tradition, a certain West Clare leprechaun found dried bird-droppings extremely good for smoking. The smoke of the pipe only adds to his overall pungency and keeps the other, more hygienic fairies away from him.

In some areas, leprechauns refuse to have their hair cut. Consequently, they are covered in long, thick, greasy strands of hair that stretch halfway down their backs. The *lengremen* of South

Armagh actually use their hair as a covering while they sleep because it is so long. However, in other parts of the country—in Galway and Kerry, for example—the leprechaun's hair seems to grow very slowly. Even so, it looks untidy and often leaves his hat reclining at a rather rakish angle—a fashion anomaly he seldom bothers to correct. The leprechaun's hair is full of leaves, twigs, and branches from the ditches and sheughs through which he has traveled.

CHAPTER 2: WHAT DO LEPRECHAUNS LOOK LIKE?

The Lepracaun; or Fairy Shoemaker
"Little Cowboy, what have you heard,
Up on the lonely rath's green mound?"
"Only the plaintive yellow bird,
Sighing in sultry fields around,
Chary, chary, chary, chee-ee!—"
"Only the grasshopper and the bee?—"
"Tip tap, rip-rap,
Tick-a-tack-too!
Scarlet leather, sewn together,
This will make a shoe.
Left, right, pull it tight;
Summer days are warm;
Underground in winter,
Laughing at the storm!"
"Lay your ear close to the hill.
Do you not catch the tiny clamour,
Busy click of an elfin hammer,
Voice of the Lepracaun singing shrill
As he merrily plies his trade?
He's a span
And a quarter in height.
Get him in sight, hold him tight,
And you're a made
Man!"

—William Allingham (1824–1889),
Irish poet, diarist, and editor

CHAPTER 3

WHERE TO FIND LEPRECHAUNS

Generally speaking, leprechauns prefer to adapt existing locations for accommodation purposes rather than to construct new dwellings from scratch. In many cases, they will use portions of extant human structures—ruined houses, old barns, even fallen church ruins. For example, a ruined church on the tiny Inner Hebridean island of Sanday was said to house one of these sprites, who was to be seen of an evening fishing from the cliffs and watching boats going to and from the Mull of Kintyre.

These church- and monastery-dwelling fairies have their roots in Northern English traditions, where they are known as "abbey lubbers": mischievous sprites who tormented lazy clergy and reminded lax and greedy monks of their vows of austerity. They also helped themselves to the abbey's finest wines. When the abbeys and monasteries fell into neglect, the abbey lubbers stayed on, frightening away anyone who came near with terrifying shrieks and strange noises.

Glaistigs

Leprechauns also made their homes in ruined castles and ancient fortresses. A number of Scottish castles are inhabited by leprechaun-like creatures known as *glaistigs*. There is some dispute as to whether these entities are male (like the leprechaun) or female, but it is generally agreed that they come from the same stock as the Irish sprite. Glaistigs were supposed to inhabit grand houses and castles, long after the human inhabitants had left.

In his book *The Peat Fire's Flame* (1937), Alasdair Alpin MacGregor mentions a particular glaistig that lived on the holy island of Iona off Scotland's west coast. Any shepherd who used the island *shielings* ("shelters") was required to pay the sprite a fee for doing so. He had to take a can of ewe's milk to "a common spot" known locally as the Glaistig's Rock, and pour it into a long crack in the surface of the stone. Failure to do this would result in some sort of *murrain* ("sickness") falling upon his flock, or in some nasty and mischievous trick being played upon the shepherd himself. No real description of this solitary fairy exists, although it is generally thought of in the same generic terms as the leprechaun and is frequently imagined to be female. Its home was believed to be within the rock, and consequently the stone could never be moved.

Eilean Mor

Similarly, on Eilean Mor, the major island in the Flannan Isles grouping west of Lewis, shepherds and wildfowlers who stayed on the island overnight had to perform a certain ritual so that a fairy force there would not torment them. According to Mary Harman, in her book on St. Kilda—*An Isle Called Hirte* (1997)—visitors to Eilean Mor had to make a circuit of the ruined chapel there on their knees, in the direction of the rising sun, praying all the while. Undoubtedly this was to protect them from a supernatural fairy creature who was said to have made his abode there and who had driven off the monks who originally built the holy site. Indeed, local shepherds who worked for MacLeod of Lewis (who owned the islands) frequently spoke of the unnatural creature who lived on Eilean Mor; they referred to the island as "the other country." In 1900, three keepers vanished from the newly constructed lighthouse there—a mystery which has never been solved—and widely believed folklore recounts that they were carried off by the fairy in the middle of a storm. The creature is not known to have any particular habitation on the small island, but is believed to dwell in the ruins of the old church.

Ruined Castles

In *Superstitions of the Highlands and Islands of Scotland* (1900), the Reverend J.G. Campbell recounts how solitary, leprechaun-like creatures also inhabit ruined castles. He cites Dunstaffnage Castle, formerly the residence of Scottish kings, as the habitation of a stunted, rather ugly fairy creature, which he describes as being female—an ell-maid. She is particularly attentive to those who stay at the castle, mischievously stripping their beds or making off with items of clothing, which are then found in some other part of the building. These, of course, are also favorite leprechaun tricks.

"The Fishermen and the Fairies"

Other such fairies are said to reside in ruined castles and churches along the Irish coast. An old story from County Limerick recounts how Irish fishermen who passed by such ruins frequently had to share their catches with the creatures, for fear of having something happen to them on the way home:

I used to hear that there was an old castle one time near Killgobban and that its stones were badly tumbled [the place lay in ruins]. A fairy had come to lodge in the place and was a great torment to all the people who lived round about. There was a fisherman called Niall Hogan who lived quite close to the place, and he used to fish every day from the rocks below the headland on which the fallen castle stood. The road down to and up from these rocks always led him past the castle, and if he had a particularly good day at the fishing, the fairy would always call out to him whenever he passed by, "Give us a wee one, Niall!" And he would have to leave a fish beside a big stone for the fairy to lift.

He noticed that the more he acceded to the fairy's requests, the more frequent and troublesome it became, sometimes demanding two or three fishes from the day's catch. He never saw the fairy, but he knew that it was there, and he could never tell whether it was male or female, for the voice sounded like both genders. The local people said it was a leprechaun and he should pay it no heed, but Niall wasn't so sure. It was better, he said, to give it the fish, in case some harm should befall him or the fish from the sea should suddenly dry up and leave him with nothing. So he left as many fish as the fairy asked for. Sometimes it pestered him so much on his way home from fishing that, by the time he had reached his own front door, he had scarcely a single fish left.

At last, a local farmer decided to destroy the old castle entirely—there's not a trace of it to be seen now—and the fairy's demands stopped. Niall was left in peace.

Old Churches

Old churches, too, were considered dwelling places of leprechauns. In many tales concerning the sprites, the consecrated ground upon which such buildings stood did not seem to bother them. At the site of an ancient monastery in South Armagh, reportedly dedicated to an obscure saint named MacCuagh, a leprechaun was supposed to have taken up his abode.

> **DARBY O'GILL**
>
> The 1959 movie *Darby O'Gill and the Little People* tells the story of an Irishman and his battle with leprechauns. The movie features Sean Connery as the love interest for Darby's daughter Katie, played by Janet Munro. The movie also features other Irish mythic creatures, such as a *pooka* (a hobgoblin) and a banshee.

"You could see him only on very bright days when the sun fell a certain way across the fields," said Minnie Murphy, a storyteller from Mullaghbawn in County Armagh. "And he would appear like a shadow, coming and going among the rays of sunlight just beyond the corner of your eye. If you looked at him directly, he was gone away among the bushes, quick as a thrush. I never saw him myself, but I was told that he was a little fellow, not any bigger than a child, and that you could never really see what he looked like. And he would call out to you sometimes, but his voice would always be like the cry of a bird away in the meadows. He spoke in an old, old language, so that you would never really understand what he was saying. And you could never really get a good look at him. But he was there, all right, even though the place was supposed to be holy ground and blessed by Saint MacCuagh himself. He hasn't been seen nor heard for a long while now. I suppose the people stopped believing in him, and he went away."

In County Tipperary, near Clonmel, a leprechaun is supposed to guard a largely disused well on the site of a former church. In this respect, he took over the function of the ancient Celtic clergy, who used to protect the well as a holy place. It was supposedly a healing well, and the priest used to live close by it in a little house, collecting donations from the pilgrims who came to be cured. When the church was abandoned, the leprechaun seems to have taken over the role of the clergy. A token would be left beside the well for the little fellow before the pilgrim used the waters. If this was not done, the cure would be ineffective or might only last for a short time. Probably the leprechaun was a memory of some ancient well-spirit, dating back to pagan times.

Leprechauns sometimes make their homes in artifacts associated with humans, as well as in ruined dwellings. For example, they might live in abandoned beehives, in the eaves of barns, in old boxes or even in discarded kettles.

Living in the Open

More commonly, however, they choose to live in the open, and there is a good reason for this. Being a sprite of the earth, the leprechaun possesses a magical power over natural things, and it is easy for him, with a little bit of "fairy glamour" (false imagery created through magic), to make his abode blend in with the existing landscape. Indeed, leprechauns are so skilled at creating illusions that a human might be standing only a few feet away from such a fairy dwelling and not be aware of its existence.

Standing Stones

As has already been mentioned in relation to the grogoch, some leprechauns choose to live in places where large standing stones provide some protection against the elements. This firmly establishes the fairy's connection with pagan sites. The fairies may also live in the depths of clumps of thornbushes or amid the roots of isolated trees, recalling the notion of tree worship in the pre-Christian era. This is why such growths are better left undisturbed by farmers or land developers.

> **THE POWER OF PRAYER**
> The only release from a fairy's spell was to turn one's coat inside out and repeat the Lord's Prayer. Only then would the fairy influence of the place be lifted.

Because of these pagan associations, many leprechauns are believed to construct their dwellings near the ancient mounds, *tumuli* ("a mound raised over a grave"), raths, and earthen forts that were raised by long-vanished peoples. Often, such places were also deemed to be the homes of the fairy folk themselves—the Macara Shee or trooping fairies—and were to be strenuously avoided. Like the fairy palaces within the raths or forts, the leprechauns' houses—so subtly blended into the landscape as to be undetectable—remained invisible to the naked human eye, and might only be seen if the person had had his or her eyes anointed with a special fairy potion or was carrying a special four-leafed shamrock or clover.

Places scattered across the fields where grass refused to grow were sometimes also considered to indicate leprechauns' houses. The building itself was believed to be invisible, but the telltale grassless patch gave away its location. However, mortals had to be careful not to inadvertently step on such areas when crossing fields or laneways, as doing so would place the traveler within the leprechaun's power. The fairy would then lead the unfortunate mortal astray, and he or she would wander for hours in a lost or dazed condition before being released from the enchantment.

Still other leprechauns chose dry caves or burrows for their homes. Such creatures are frequently described as being what we might call "taller" fairies—"about the height of a child of two or three"—but still much smaller than mortals.

Isle of Lewis Chessmen

In 1831, a laborer who was walking along the seashore near Uig, on the Isle of Lewis, noticed that some very bad weather had washed away a large sandbank, exposing the entrance to a small, low cave. Curiosity got the better of him; he poked his head into the opening and saw, to his amazement, a large beehive-shaped dwelling made out of clay, deep in the interior of the cave. Thinking there might be treasure in it, left over from the Viking occupation of the island, he smashed a section of it open.

Suddenly, the air was filled with a kind of angry crying, like a thousand voices mixed with the low drone of bees. Terrified that he had destroyed part of a leprechaun's or brownie's home, the laborer dropped his implements and ran.

When he returned home, his wife, who was made of much sterner stuff than he, made him go back and investigate further. Peering into the queer structure, he found a number of objects that he originally thought were Little People. These were in fact a full set of ninety-three chess pieces, exquisitely carved from walrus ivory. They are now on display in the British Museum as the Lewis chessmen (reproductions of them are on sale everywhere), and historians have dated them to the eleventh or twelfth century.

Some of the Lewis Islanders, however, tell a different story. These chessmen are the work of a fairy sculptor who once dwelt on the island—a leprechaun-like figure who lived alone among the sand dunes. And who is to say that this is not the truth of it?

Hedge Leprechauns

The smaller types of leprechaun most often live in gullies or "*sheughs*," particularly where the hedges have grown down to give protection. It is particularly difficult to investigate these places, for the leprechaun will pick the most inaccessible area of the drain in which to establish his house, and so the investigator will be torn and mauled by brambles and thorns while trying to see the leprechaun dwelling and will probably end up not seeing anything at all.

A sure signal that a leprechaun is concealed somewhere along a gully or drain is said to be the tapping sound which he makes while working at a pair of brogues or other shoes. If a mortal coming too close to his house disturbs the leprechaun, he will abandon the shoe and scamper back into his abode. Consequently, a small number of storytellers are able to produce discarded shoes leprechauns have left behind. The most famous of these was the folklorist W.J. Fitzpatrick, who lived in the Mourne Mountains of County Down in the early part of the twentieth century. A photograph of a discarded fairy shoe that he kept in his possession was printed in the *Mourne Observer* in the 1950s, but since the photo was taken, the shoe has mysteriously disappeared.

> ### LEPRECHAUN HUNT
> In 1989 in the Irish town of Carlingford, a pub owner claims to have heard a scream from a well. Investigating, he found a tiny set of bones and some clothing he identified as belonging to a leprechaun. He put them on display, where they attracted so much attention that the town now sponsors an annual leprechaun hunt. Adults who take part in the hunt are given a small bottle of whiskey to assist them in their search for the wee folk.

Avoid Leprechaun Hospitality

Although leprechauns' houses are often hard to find, sometimes mortals will stumble upon them by accident. If this should occur, the mortal must never, under any circumstances, accept hospitality from the sprite, as severe repercussions are bound to ensue. The following story comes from the Bog of Allen, in the South East Midlands, and serves as a warning of such consequences.

CHAPTER 3: WHERE TO FIND LEPRECHAUNS

"The Girl Who Stayed Too Long"

There was a girl who one time had gone to a fair with a young man on whom she was very sweet. On the way home, they fell out—as lovers will sometimes do—and, in a fit of temper, she jumped down from the donkey cart he was driving and stormed off along the road. He, being in an equally bad temper, drove on home without her, shouting that a good walk would do her no harm and would serve to cool her passion and stay her bad tongue.

The thing was that she had jumped from the cart in the middle of a bog, and was forced to walk along long and lonely roads without ever meeting a single person. Ah, but there's a warning to us all there, not to be so hasty in our words and actions!

Soon night was coming down upon her and she was nowhere near her home. There was a smurr ("a slight drizzle") of rain on the wind as well, and, having no head covering and fearing a bit of a storm, she looked around for some sort of shelter. Away out in the bog, she saw the light of a window, and she thought that she might go there and ask for a wee bit of shelter for the night. Then she could set out for home again in the morning.

There was only a peat road leading into the bog toward the light, and it was badly grown about with reeds and rushes and spiky bushes. All the same, the girl forced her way on toward the light, and just as the sun was going down, she came upon a little house of sod built in the very heart of the bog, with a bit of an old haw-lantern in its window. And sitting in front of its open door on a three-legged stool was a wee man, no bigger than a two-year-old child, smoking an old dudeen in the last of the evening. Beside him on the ground lay an old fiddle and bow. He was warming himself in front of a small fire that he had lit in front of his doorway.

He looked up at her as she came out of the dark, and she saw that his skin was tanned and weather-beaten and that his hair and beard were as black as coal. But it was his eyes, which were quick and intelligent, that took her interest.

She Asks for Shelter

She told him that she was a traveler who was a long way from home, and that she would be grateful if he would let her lie by his fire for the night and share his family's meal.

The little man looked at her queerly. "I live here alone," says he, with a queer accent in his tone that reminded her of Old Irish. "But you are welcome to share what I have. I must tell you that I am a bit of a musician, and that on nights such as this, my neighbors, who also live in this bog, will gather here for a bit of a céilí ("dance"). But you are welcome to join in with us if you have a mind to, for there will not be much sleeping done this night."

Now the girl was always ready for a céilí, and she readily agreed. The little old man beckoned her into the house, and when she got into the place, she found out just how low it was. She could barely stand up in it, and there appeared to be no furniture about it at all—just a few old seats and a table. The floor had been swept quite clean, though, as if ready for some merriment.

The man produced an old jug of poteen and the two of them went outside to enjoy the night. Gradually, other people began to come out of the twilight from different directions across the bog. Not one of them was any bigger than a child, although they all appeared to be very old, and the girl noticed that she was the only woman among them. Every one of them was a little old man.

Her host lifted his fiddle and began a merry tune, and soon the céilí was in full swing, away in that remote and lonely place. The girl so enjoyed the music that she got up to dance, and soon she was leaping with the best of them around the fire at the doorway of the small house.

She danced and danced until it seemed that she would never stop; as soon as she had finished dancing with one of the small men, another would step up to take his place. And every time she paused for breath, someone would come forward with a cup of poteen for her. She would gulp it down and dance some more. She danced until her feet were numb and she was exhausted—so exhausted that she collapsed in a heap, just in front of the doorway to the house of sod.

The Next Day

She awoke in the middle of the bog, with nobody next to nor near her. Of the house, the fire, and the noisy company, there was no sign. She lay with her head almost in a bog hole and a fearsome pain in her feet. When she looked down, she saw they were covered in blood. Indeed, she had danced so much that her feet were raw and she had almost danced her toes off. It was only then that she realized she had been dancing all night with the leprechauns of the bog, those tireless dancers who fade away on the wind as soon as the sun is up.

Getting up, she limped back to the road and eventually made her way home. When she came near her own house, she began to notice how things had changed. On the road, near to her own gate, she met a couple of people coming down toward her. She looked at them and they at her, but neither recognized the other. And the houses were different, too—where there should have been thatch, there was now slate, and where the walls should have been whitewashed with lime, they were now dashed with pebbles. And she passed houses by the roadside that she never remembered seeing before. It was all very strange. The people working in the fields seemed different too. There were young people that she should have known but didn't recognize, and the fields that had been boggy and rushy when she had left the previous morning were now flat and cultivated, with cattle grazing in them or crops growing there.

At length she came to her own gateway, and right glad she was to see it, for her poor feet were in agony. She hobbled up to the door, but as she did so, a strange woman came to the door and asked her what she wanted.

"I want to come into my own house!" said the girl rather angrily.

The woman just looked at her in astonishment. "I don't know who you are," she said, with a stiff tone in her voice, "nor what you think you're doing, but this is not your house!" She said it with such finality that the girl knew she wasn't lying. "Now get away from my door, old woman, and be about your business."

The Voice from the Past

The girl looked at her, aghast. Who was this cheeky besom ("loose woman") who referred to her as "old woman"? The woman at the door looked old enough to be her mother!

"This is indeed my house!" she told her. "At least, it was when I left here this morning. And who are you, anyway, to come claiming it for your own?"

The woman gave her a look of distaste. "I have lived here with my husband these last twenty years," she told the astonished girl. "And before me it was a family named Mulligan, who moved away to Ballina in the County Mayo. And long before that it was a family named Cosendine..."

The girl gasped. "But that's my name!" she told the strange woman. "I'm Kate Cosendine."

The woman looked at her curiously for a moment, then made the sign of the cross in the air above her head. "Lord help me!" she cried, stepping back into the cottage. "You're Kitty Cosendine who vanished all those years ago, on her way home from the fair with Dan Sullivan. I mind my grandmother telling me about it, for it all happened when she was a child herself."

Kitty sat down on the edge of the doorstep, a great weariness suddenly overcoming her.

"Look at yourself, woman!" And the woman of the house fetched a mirror so Kitty could see herself.

What she saw looking back at her was the face of an old, old woman, dirty like a beggar-hag, with straggly gray hair and the lines of great age all across her withered skin. Gone was the young girl who had left home all those years ago—years that had passed in a single night's dancing with the leprechauns out in the bog.

PEAT

In some wetland areas of Ireland, vegetation decays in a form called peat. It can be cut and put on a fire, where it burns slowly, making it a good fuel for a land with few trees.

The woman drove Kitty away from her door, and for most of the day she wandered the roads, hearing bits of stories about herself—for the legend of Kitty Cosendine was well known in the locality. It appeared that Dan Sullivan had waited for her for many years but had eventually married another girl. His grandchildren still lived nearby. Her family had fallen on hard times and had been forced to move on, and now no trace of them remained in the countryside.

There was nowhere for Kitty to go and no one to take her in. Her feet ached, but she had to keep walking; she had no rest at all.

As evening drew on, she approached the church. Dragging herself up the steps, she peered in through the door. A service was in progress and the priest was in the very act of elevating the host. And as he called God's blessing on all present, Kitty Cosendine fell away to dust with a final sigh. She had found her rest at last.

But her story is a warning to one and all against accepting the hospitality of the leprechauns, or of any other fairy creature. Their ways are not our ways; neither is their time like ours. Those who sit by the fires of the Sídhe may find that their time has already passed without them realizing it.

Rushy Men

It was not always easy to recognize fairy houses, and humans were wont to stumble upon them by accident. Bogs and mosses throughout the countryside were frequently the home of leprechauns, harking back to an old meaning of the name—"rushy man." Their huts were either of peat cut from the bog itself or of rushes and grass tied into intricate designs. In the evening, the voices of the leprechauns could be heard crying from their secret houses among the rushes, the sounds high and shrill like those of waterfowl. Cynics may very well say these are no more than the cries of birds nesting in the bogs, but the wise man is not always so dismissive. It would be folly, however, to follow such cries in order to see the leprechaun: the sounds might lead you into the most dangerous part of the swamp, and you might never find your way out again or sink into the mud without a trace. Hunting leprechauns in such terrain is a dangerous business indeed.

CHAPTER 4

WHAT DO THEY EAT AND DRINK?

The leprechaun is usually described as a "fairy shoemaker," but, as we shall see later, this is not always true. Many leprechauns do not need to work, as they often know the whereabouts of ancient treasure that can keep them in the manner to which they wish to become accustomed. Some of them do not work at all. And perhaps it is just as well, for most leprechauns have an inherent weakness: they are all exceptionally fond of strong drink, particularly poteen.

To say that illicit spirits are an integral part of leprechaun culture would be something of an understatement. Indeed, much of the leprechaun's day revolves around the manufacture and consumption of the same. The leprechaun's constitution must be an extremely sturdy one, for not only does the creature consume staggering amounts of liquor (enough to render several battalions of strong mortal men senseless), but the concoction he drinks is so impure that it would be positively fatal to mortals. As has already been stated, hygiene is not a big consideration in the leprechaun's world, and this lack of cleanliness is often evident in the distilling process.

Distilling from Anything

The leprechaun will use almost any abandoned mortal domestic utensil as a basis for his "still"—an old pot, an earthen jar, a kettle coated in rust. The impurities the raw spirit might absorb from these vessels appear to be of little concern to him, as long as the end result can be drunk. He will distill his spirit from all sorts of available rubbish—old potato peelings, bits of old turnip, carrots, and so on—as well as from the conventional barley grain.

In most cases, leprechauns do not distill for profit (in other words, they do not sell the results of their efforts—although a very few may do so on occasion); they prepare the majority of their brews for their own consumption. Consequently, few of them are seen without a quart jug somewhere nearby, from which they will take a swig from time to time.

RAISE A GLASS

Although it was illegal for centuries in Ireland to distill poteen, as of 2008 it has become legal (although it's still illegal in Northern Ireland). According to European Union regulations, all real poteen must come from Ireland. It's brewed in a small pot; the Irish word for such a pot is *pota*. Hence the name of the drink.

The sprite's occupation of ruined castles and houses adds to the availability of distilling space, and old cupboards or niches can quickly be converted into areas in which spirit production can take place. As well as manufacturing spirits, the leprechaun is also extremely adept at preparing wines, ales, and beers, which he drinks with consummate gusto. Despite the large quantities of liquor he imbibes, and despite the fact that he is often extremely tipsy, the leprechaun is seldom so drunk that he can be easily caught by a mortal hunter or by a scavenging animal or bird. Even in an inebriated state, he can still move with surprising speed and alacrity.

Human Drink

Leprechauns also enjoy drink that has been spilled from human glasses. Some leprechauns will sit invisibly in public houses, trying to jog the elbows of the drinkers so they will spill a sup of stout or a small measure of whiskey for the leprechaun's convenience. If a drop is spilled, it is customary to say, "Here's a drop for you, little fellow," to ensure good luck on the coming day. If it is cleaned up too hastily (that is, before the leprechaun can sup it up), misfortune may descend not only upon the individual drinker but upon the licensed establishment.

The sprites will also hang around the doorways of houses in the hope that some drink will accidentally be spilled inside. This holds a number of grave dangers for them. The foremost of these is that the owner of the house may throw out water at the end of the day, drenching the little fellow as he waits invisibly in the evening light. If this happens, the leprechaun is, understandably, not best pleased, and he may take some form of revenge against the household concerned. It is therefore prudent to shout a warning before throwing water out into the dusk. A common warning might be *"Hugitas, ugitas, uisce salach!"* ("Away, away, dirty water!") Upon hearing this, all fairy creatures know to withdraw from the immediate vicinity of the door for fear of being splashed.

LUCKY LEPRECHAUN

For those looking for a leprechaun-themed drink, this is something to try on St. Patrick's Day.

- 1 fluid ounce Southern Comfort
- ½ fluid ounce Midori melon liqueur
- ½ fluid ounce Malibu rum
- 6 fluid ounces pineapple juice
- 1 dash blue curaçao
- 1 lime wedge

Mix all liquids in glass or shaker and pour over ice. Garnish with lime wedge.

Leprechauns are not terribly partial to other human drinks such as tea or coffee, although they will sample a cup if there is nothing else available. It is thought that the caffeine in both beverages will bring out itchy welts and blotches, similar to hives in a human being, and will leave the fairy feeling uncomfortable. If all else fails, the leprechaun will drink spring water (but not tap water), although he will do so with an ill grace, muttering and complaining all the while. Leprechauns and water are not terribly compatible. He will do his best to avoid fizzy drinks such as soda, as these will make him bloated and queasy. It is therefore better for him to stick to supping poteen—the drink he knows best.

Food

Generally speaking, leprechauns will eat roughly the same food as humans. The few accounts we have of fairy food suggest that it is not terribly substantial or filling, and while it may suit the trooping fairies—who are always very fussy about their figures—it is hardly fit for a hungry leprechaun who has no such worries. However, his tastes are very plain, and he will not eat sweet biscuits or fancy side dishes, simply because he does not like them. Nor will he touch processed food, so cans of beans, peas, or pasta in tomato sauce are practically poison to him. Being a traditionalist, he is wary of any sort of foreign food. Curries, kebabs, and Chinese food are all anathema to him, although a few of the sprites have been known to eat the topping off pizza (but only if it is made with fresh tomatoes and cheese).

Traditionally speaking, the leprechaun is known to consume large quantities of potatoes, washed down with either poteen or sweet milk. He is also partial to the occasional side of beef or chicken leg when he can get them, and he has been known to raid the larders of sleeping mortals in order to obtain these delicacies.

Crumbs from the Table

Generally, the leprechaun contents himself with whatever crumbs and scraps he can take from the tables of humans. If a morsel of food falls to the ground, it immediately becomes his property and should not be retrieved. In certain parts of Ireland—for example, Connemara—crusts of bread, and other pieces of food that had been discarded or dropped, were traditionally placed on a convenient window ledge as a kind of "offering" to the leprechauns.

There are, however, a number of delicacies which are specific to leprechauns and detrimental to mortals. For example, leprechauns, like many other fairies, find mushrooms and other fungi of varying types particularly tasty.

Fungi

Toadstools, in particular, are often the basis of the leprechauns' nourishing broths (nourishing to them, that is, since most humans would find such a concoction extremely poisonous). And among their most famous foods is the so-called "fairy butter," a soft, cheese-like fungus that grows on the boles of very old trees. This is the central ingredient in most fairy cookery—particularly baking. On no account should a human eat this mold, for it will be found to be at best almost tasteless, at worst poisonous. In the fairy world, however, this butter is used both as a condiment and as a relish, and leprechauns keep great stores of it near their dwellings—so if a mortal comes across the fungus growing at the base of a tree, there is sure to be a leprechaun's house somewhere close by.

The roots of the silverweed, too, are especially sought after by the little men. They are used as the basis of many soups and stews, which the sprites prepare in small iron pots. It is thought that these roots were once the staple food of Irish mortals, who gave up eating them as soon as potatoes were imported from the New World.

Heather

Heather is used in leprechaun cuisine to thicken stews and gravies on the sprite's table; it can also be brewed into a fine beer which can be drunk along with the meal. The secret of making heather beer was once known to all, but over the years it was forgotten, and it is now one of the most famous "lost arts" of Ireland. It was certainly still known to two old Viking brothers who lived in Donegal in the mid-twelfth century, but upon their deaths it was forgotten and so lost. Now only the leprechauns remember the recipe. Heather stems are sometimes also served as sweetmeats at the end of a meal—a kind of digestif for cleansing both the palate and the teeth.

Although the leprechaun finds food pleasant to eat, it is not essential to him. As long as he eats once in a while, he can go for days without partaking of any such nourishment. Poteen is more essential to him than a staple diet!

CHAPTER 5

ARE THERE FEMALE LEPRECHAUNS?

Throughout this text, the Irish leprechaun has been referred to as "he," and there is a good reason for this. Although some folklorists may disagree, there is no substantive evidence for the existence of female leprechauns in Ireland. Niall Macnamara, in his book *The Leprechaun Companion* (1999), mentions a female of the species but gives little indication as to where she may be found. General opinion, however, noting the inherent solitary nature of the leprechaun, makes no mention of either marriage or courtship. He is portrayed as an isolated bachelor, with no female companion or counterpart.

Grogochs

This impression may not be strictly true, for the matter is complicated by the inclusion of the Scottish grogoch in the leprechaun classification. On the Isle of Arran in the Firth of Clyde, grogochs are always considered female. A further complication is added by the definition of a Highland grogoch: this is a witch/wizard who has shape-shifting abilities and may change his other form and gender at will. In Brittany, the fées and *lutins* (little leprechaun-like spirits who either live in the wild or attach themselves to the houses of certain families) are usually considered to be female. However, in Ireland, the leprechaun is believed to be male.

Leprechaun Reproduction

This notion leads to the inevitable question: how do leprechauns reproduce?

This is a problem that has never been satisfactorily answered, for the leprechaun is understandably reluctant to discuss the matter. A creature of utmost secrecy, he cannot be coaxed or cajoled into revealing anything regarding his courtship or reproductive practices.

There are, however, a number of theories as to how leprechauns came to be.

Most leprechauns claim to be directly descended from the Tuatha dé Danann, who are said to have arrived in Ireland around the third millennium B.C.E. However, there seems to be little basis for this claim. Almost every source describes the Tuatha dé Danann arriving in clouds from the east and settling on a mountain in the west of Ireland, causing a great eclipse of the sun as they did so. They were, say the ancient accounts, an extremely advanced, learned, industrious, and exceptionally tall and beautiful people. Some folklorists have compared them to the ancient Greeks. The leprechaun, on the other hand, is small and stunted, rather ugly, and in no way advanced or learned. Therefore, his relationship to the Tuatha dé Danann is extremely tenuous.

However, this is not to deny that there may be some sort of connection, for some folklorists have described the leprechaun as an offshoot (or "by-blow") of the Tuatha dé Danann lineage.

> **CONQUERORS AND RULERS**
> The Tuatha dé Danann fought and conquered tribes in Ireland when they first came there. They defeated the Fir Bolg at the battle of Magh Tuireadh. After ruling for many years, they fought many battles against the invading Milesians. Finally the two sides compromised; the Milesians ruled the upper world, and the Tuatha dé Danann ruled the land of the Underworld.

It is well known throughout the Celtic world that fairy women find the process of giving birth extremely difficult. This is probably due to the fact that this event happens infrequently. Having no midwives of their own, they are forced to labor as best they can, or to employ the services of a human midwife who has greater knowledge of the birthing process. Stories of midwives in remote areas of the country being carried off by fairies to assist at a birth are found all over Ireland, from Donegal to Kerry, and in many other Celtic lands.

The Fairy Child

When the fairy child is born, it sometimes appears to be a small, wizened, ugly thing, which bears little or no resemblance to its often stately and beautiful parents. In most of the folktales, it is hustled away before the midwife can see it and seems to disappear from the story. Folklorists have suggested that these stunted and repulsive children form the basis of the leprechaun population. They are cast out of the fairy host, to become either changelings (sickly and complaining fairies who are sometimes left in the place of stolen human children) or the surly, dudeen-smoking sprites of the leprechaun clans. The fact that the leprechaun is, in fact, more or less an outcast from the mainstream fairy world is often cited as a reason for his sullen and antisocial nature, as well as for his elusive habits.

All leprechauns, says this theory, are male because the proportion of stunted or deformed male children is much higher in the fairy world than it is in the human world (female fairies are always born radiant and beautiful, with no blemishes whatsoever), and their numbers are added to practically every time a fairy woman gives birth. There is no real evidence for this theory, as none of the stunted fairy offspring have ever been traced and there are no stories of them beyond their births. However, it remains one of the most plausible accounts of the origins of the leprechaun.

CHANGELINGS

There exists in Ireland and Scotland the tradition of the changeling—the fairy child substituted in the cradle for a human child, who was taken away to live with the fairies. For this reason, it was dangerous to praise a baby too much, as this might attract the attention of the fairy folk. Parents could guard against such fey abductions by turning the baby's clothing inside out or dangling needles or scissors from the crib.

Fairy-Human Unions

Another theory is that the leprechaun is the product of an illicit union between a fairy and a human. From time to time, according to legend, certain mortals and members of the fairy folk met together as lovers, even though the church had expressly banned any form of consorting between the two. The product of this union was a small, stunted being—not quite human, but not quite fairy either—who would eventually become a form of dwarf.

Certainly these human-fairy unions were quite common in former times in Ireland, particularly among great and heroic men. The Irish hero Dunlaing O'Hartigan, one of the foremost captains in Brian Boru's army at the Battle of Clontarf in 1014, is said to have lain with the fairy woman Aoibheall and had a son by her. Before the battle, Aoibheall appeared in Brian's camp and promised Dunlaing and his mortal sons two hundred years of life if they would put off fighting for one day. She told him that if he did not, he would be slain the next day, and she reminded the captain that they had an infant son—half human, half fairy—for whom he was responsible. Being a warrior, O'Hartigan refused, and he and his sons were killed the following day in a fierce battle against the Norsemen. Aoibheall eventually became a banshee—reputedly one of the first in Ireland—on the slopes above Lough Derg. No further mention is made of the half-human child, and some have argued that it might have become a leprechaun-like figure.

"The Fairy Mother"

A similar story comes from an old folktale from Urlaur Lough in County Mayo. Here, it is said, a fairy came to the door of St. Thomas's Church, near the shores of the lough, to plead with her former partner to acknowledge their offspring.

PART I: WHO ARE THE LITTLE PEOPLE?

The priest had just begun his homily, and all eyes were fixed upon him, when outside the wind began to rise, like the scream of a thousand voices, and the day seemed to darken slightly beyond the church windows. The congregation shuffled and muttered among themselves uneasily, but the priest continued with his sermon, although his voice seemed to falter slightly.

Then, over the shriek of the wind, came another voice which drowned out the drone of the priest. It seemed to be the cry of a woman in torment: "Come out! Come out!" And it named the son of a local gentleman, who sat in the congregation. "Come out and acknowledge what is truly yours." The cry was accompanied by a hammering on the church doors which sounded like a roll of thunder.

All heads turned, but the young man sat with a stony face beside his father, looking fixedly toward the altar.

Again the voice cried, "Come out! I call on you to come from that place and take what is yours!" Again there was the fearful hammering. Even the priest had stopped now, but still nobody made any move.

At last the priest stepped down and walked to the heavy oaken doors of the church, to see who was calling. Throwing the doors wide, he looked out into the dark day.

A beautiful woman stood there, but the holy man could see by her great loveliness and her strange, pale complexion that this was no earthly person. She was one of the Sídhe, who had come down from the rath nearby to beat on the church doors. In the crook of her left arm she held a small bundle, and as the priest watched, a tiny arm poked from its coverings and waved in the air.

There was a child in that bundle, thought the astonished cleric. He made the sign of the cross in the air, to protect against fairy magic. The woman seemed to shrink back slightly, still clutching her bundle tightly.

"What is it that you want in the house of God?" intoned the priest.

The woman drew herself up to her full height, and the child gurgled in its wrappings. "I am come here so that the father of my child can own what is his," said she, "and so that I can then present my infant, as the fruit of his loins, for the holy baptism of the mortal world."

The priest stood aghast. "Surely you know that it is unlawful in the eyes of our Mother Church for one of your kind to have relations with the children of Adam, for whom Christ died? No Christian man could have fathered this child."

No Pity for the Fairy Child

The woman looked at him with tears brimming in her large and lovely eyes. "Spoken like a man of the cloth," she replied. "Spoken without a shred of pity. Well, priest, let me tell you this. This man"—and she named him again—"is the father of this child—Christian or no Christian. Let him come forward and deny it to my face—the face of the woman who loved him and who loves him yet. And if he does so, then I must abandon my own child, for that is the decree of those who dwell within my rath. He will have not only my own woe upon his shoulders, but also the woes of the son who has his blood within his veins. Will he deny the cry of his own human blood? Let him come to the door and face me now!"

The priest hesitated. "It is also against the decree of our Holy Mother Church for a clergyman to barter with one of the Sídhe," he said at length. "But you accuse me of having no pity. I will therefore do as you ask. I will call the man that you have named to the door of the church and let him either own or deny the child. I do it not to satisfy you but for the sake of the infant in your arms. The Lord Christ Himself shows mercy to the smallest child—maybe even to those of the Sídhe—and who am I to do otherwise?"

He turned back into the chapel and called out the young man's name, instructing him to come forward to the church door. The boy came forward hesitantly, and there was an air of slyness about him. His father followed him out of the dark interior of the church and stood behind him as he faced the fairy woman and her child. The priest also stood by, his right hand on the baptismal font which stood just inside the door.

The Father Rejects His Child

The boy blinked in the harsh daylight after the cool gloom of the church, but gave not the slightest sign that he recognized the fairy.

"I am come to the door of the church," he said, glancing at his father out of the corner of his eye. "What is it that you want with me?"

In reply, the fairy gave a kind of low wail and held out the child, still gurgling merrily in his wrap. "Only acknowledge what is yours," she pleaded, "so that he may be baptized in the fashion of the White Christ. Only then has he any hope of entering Heaven. Oh, only acknowledge your own son, even if you do not acknowledge me!"

The boy paused uncertainly. He stole a glance at his father, who stood almost behind him on his left, and then at the priest, who stood to his right. Words paused on his lips. The child laughed and crowed in the few rays of sunlight that were falling between the dark clouds overhead.

"Well?" asked the priest. "Is this truly your child? Have you been consorting with this woman, against all the dictates of the Church?"

For a moment there was silence, but at last the boy spoke.

"How can I acknowledge one of the fairy kind as my own?" he demanded. "This has nothing to do with me. It is a trick of the Sídhe, a ploy to get one of their loathly kind to enter Heaven through the sacrament of baptism. Take yourself away, woman, for I know neither yourself nor your brat. I am engaged to be married and would not have you ruin me with your lies. Return to your rath, and trouble me and my family no more!"

He spoke sharply and cruelly, and at his words, the fairy woman gave a terrible howl of despair.

"One thousand years have I lived in the world," she screamed, "and in all that time I have seen nothing so heartless as a father who will deny his own child! By the cruelty of your words, you have denied your son a place among the angels in Heaven and have turned me out from my own rath and my own people. Your soul is doubly damned!"

The boy, however, was not to be moved. "Go!" he shouted. "You have shamed both me and my family by your baseless accusations. I will hear you no more, nor will I acknowledge your fairy brat as my own son!"

The priest stepped forward. "You have heard what the son of Adam has said," he rebuked the fairy. "Now be on your way, and trouble my congregation no further!"

Dramatically, he raised his hand and pointed her away from the door of the chapel. The boy and his father turned back into the church.

The fairy's grief was awesome to behold. Overhead, the sky darkened with tempestuous clouds, and a shrill wind began to rise from the direction of the lough. It whipped around the walls of the venerable building, wailing like a banshee, rattling at the windows as though demanding entrance. A finger of lightning flickered in the sky overhead, and thunder boomed far off in the distance with a terrible sound.

The Fairy's Revenge

The fairy woman lifted the child above her head. He screamed fiercely, but she held him in an iron grip.

"If you will not accept my child freely by baptism into your mortal world," she cried, "then take it without my blessing. It shall never be accepted by the lords of the Sídhe, so let it lie among the followers of the White Christ." And so saying, she threw the child through the door of the church, directly at the font by the priest's hand.

The infant screamed loudly. As he struck the font with a loud crack, he dissolved into a cloud of smoke, which dissipated throughout the church. As all eyes were fixed upon him, no one was looking at the fairy woman; but when they turned to her again, she too had vanished.

The day, however, remained dark and gloomy, with ominous, rolling clouds. And when the font was examined, it was found to have a large crack along one side, as if it had been struck by a heavy weight.

It is said that the church was reconsecrated because of the contamination by the strange smoke which had blown through it, and that a new baptismal font was put in; the old one was thrown away. Never again did a fairy come to the doors of the church; but, by the same token, neither the boy who had been accused of fathering the child nor his own father ever prospered again. They lost money, and eventually they had to sell their land and move away. That's what comes of being involved too closely with the fairies.

The previous story has a number of variations all over Ireland. One variant, which was at one time particularly widespread, comes from Hilltown in County Down, and for many years local people could name the family involved, as they still lived in the district. The cracked baptismal font remained for some time, well outside the precincts of the local church. In County Mayo, however, the story has an especial resonance, as St. Thomas's Church near Urlaur Lough was believed to have been possessed by the Devil, who had to be driven out by a drunken piper from County Clare named Donagh O'Grady. It was widely believed in this area that both the Evil One and dark fairies still lingered close by and were ready to tempt mortals at every conceivable opportunity. In some accounts, the church is said to have been a Protestant one, and the name of the young man concerned is given as Robert Ormsby, who was later a miserly landlord and priest hunter in the area. The Ormsbys were believed to have dealt frequently with the fairies, who had many children by them.

Fairy Children

These and other accounts also contain a suggestion that fairy women actively sought out male partners from the mortal world so any offspring might have a chance of Heaven. All fairies were denied entrance to Paradise due to the fact that they had no souls and had not received Christian baptism. The gates of Heaven, however, stood open to all baptized mortals. Even though the heavenly pleasures were denied to them, many fairy women felt their offspring might attain Paradise if they had at least some human blood in their veins. By having a human father—if this was acknowledged—the infant could also lay claim to a human baptism, which would secure entrance to Paradise at the end of all things.

However, since it was against the laws of the church to consort with fairies, many human fathers refused to acknowledge their fairy children and rebuffed their former lovers, as in the previous tale. The children, neither wholly fairy nor wholly human, could not be accepted by the fairy kind in their raths and mounds and so were turned out to fend for themselves in the wider world. They were forced to live alone, well away from the main fairy habitations, and to make their own way as best they could. These abandoned fairy children, it has been argued, formed the basis of the leprechaun belief.

The frequency of alleged unions between humans and fairies, which gave rise to large numbers of offspring, may give some credence to the idea that the leprechaun is a kind of "halfling," caught somewhere between the two species. Certainly, he has some attributes that might be considered the result of human parentage.

Hair Color

First, there is his hair color. Many leprechauns are described as red-haired, with a certain ruddiness about them. Red is not a color that occurs naturally in the fairy world. Indeed, the color red is often considered an anathema to both fairies and witches. In many parts of Ireland and Scotland, strands of red thread were woven into the tails of grazing cattle to prevent fairies (or local witches) from stealing their milk, while red ribbon or red thread entwined with straw ("the straw halter") was placed around the neck of a churn during the butter-making process to prevent the fairies from stealing the produce. Celtic people, however, were often red-haired, and the leprechaun's hair color is therefore suggestive of a union that is not within the fairy world, but rather between fairy and human.

Other leprechauns have occasionally been described as fair-haired. Again, blond hair is unusual in the fairy world, and this coloring may be representative of the Viking settlers who inhabited parts of Ireland during the ninth, tenth, and eleventh centuries. While the majority of these settlers dwelt in largely enclosed city-states—Dublin, Waterford, Wexford, Limerick, Cork, and so on—there is much evidence that they did in fact marry outside the perimeters of such areas, mostly among the local Irish and others. This gave rise to a race of people in both Ireland and Scotland known as "Gael-Goidl" (foreign Gaels), and it may be that the leprechaun is somehow related to this particular race, as his hair color may denote.

Complexion

Second, there is the question of the leprechaun's general complexion. He is frequently described as ugly or rough-looking, with swarthy skin. This is in contrast to the Tuatha dé Danann, who are described as graceful, fine-featured, pale or golden-skinned, and beautiful. It has been suggested that the Tuatha dé Danann might have been of Greek origin (as they came from the east) and may have had classical Greek features. This, again, is in marked contrast to the leprechaun's general appearance, suggesting that the sprite has his origins in some subspecies of fairy (who perhaps came from somewhere other than Ireland) or in the human world.

Temperament

Third, there is the matter of the leprechaun's temperament and his general isolation from the majority of the fairy world. While he is certainly not the only fairy who might be regarded as solitary—the banshee, the pooka, and the dullahan are also so regarded (although these beings may be more closely allied to the worlds of ghosts and demons than the world of the fairies)—he is undoubtedly the most notable. Some of the possible reasons for his isolation have already been mentioned, but there is little doubt that both his manners and his way of life also serve to alienate him from the more homogeneous fairy throng. The leprechaun is a loner and has little time for the frivolities and intrigues of the localized fairy courts.

Life in the fairy mounds is said to be "gracious and languid" and "one of great ease." In each mound, a local fairy king and his queen are supposedly adored by their court, though one gathers that the fairy courts are not all that different from those of the human world. Both contain their spats, jealousies, and rivalries between courtiers; both are places of great intrigue, rumor, and gossip; and both are places where individual courtiers flit in and out of favor. The fairy court is, in fact, noted for its capricious nature and its shallowness. It is also noted for its idleness. The leprechaun, of course, has little time for this, for his disposition is very different from that of the fairy courtier.

LEPRECHAUNS AND FAIRIES

The trooping fairies regard the leprechaun as dirty, rough, vulgar, and uncouth, while he in turn considers them fickle, shallow, feckless, stupid, and idle. Contact between the two branches of fairydom is kept to a minimum—although there are occasions when communication between them is essential. The fairy throng lives for the praise and approval of others, while the leprechaun needs no such flattery.

These great differences in temperament, style, and outlook may indicate a difference in origins. The leprechaun is thought to come from a more pragmatic stock (which may have contained some human elements), while the fairy kind of the mounds and raths may be direct descendants of the ancient Tuatha dé Danann.

This theory does not explain the preponderance of males in the leprechaun line. It may be that some races tend to produce more male offspring than female (just as some human families do), and this may account for the large male leprechaun populace.

However, as has already been intimated, there are female creatures which—while not counted as leprechauns by purists—exhibit some of the traits that characterize the leprechaun world. It is to these creatures that we must now turn our attention.

Female Leprechaun Creatures

Because many fairies are shape-shifters with the ability to take on the form of any person or creature they please, the notion of gender in the fairy world has always been slightly problematic. Nevertheless, we can make some form of gender generalizations about some of the leprechaun-like sprites that inhabit this realm.

The grogoch is a North Antrim leprechaun who is often overly helpful to farmers and housewives in that area. In Antrim, the creature is invariably male, but this is not the case everywhere. On the Isle of Arran and in the Western Highlands, the being is exclusively female. In his book *The Supernatural Highlands* (1997), Francis Thompson writes:

"[The gruagach] is a female spectre of the class of brownies to which Highland dairymaids made frequent libations of fresh milk. She frisked and gambolled about the cattle pens and folds, armed only with a pliable reed, with which she switched all who annoyed her by uttering obscene language, or by neglecting to leave for her a share of the dairy produce. In Gaelic, *gruagach* is a word meaning 'wizard-champion' and is, strangely, masculine."

The Gruagach and Cattle

The main function of the gruagach, Thompson writes, is to preside over the cattle and take an interest in matters pertaining to them. A description given by a woman on the island of Heisgeir, off North Uist, who saw the gruagach moving about by the light of the moon, states she has a full conical hat and a rich mantle of golden hair falling down around her shoulders, and with a slight swish of her wand she could skillfully admonish some nearby cow. She was habitually seen (and heard) on the grounds of an old nunnery, where her melodious voice sang snatches of an eerie song that was carried about the island on the wind.

The *New Statistical Account for Scotland* (1842), dealing with the parish of Kilmuir in Skye, states:

> "Even so late as 1770, the dairymaids who attended a herd of cattle on the island of Trodda were in the habit of pouring daily a quantity of milk in a hollow stone for the gruagach. Should they neglect to do so, they were sure of feeling the effects of the brownie the next day. It is said that the Reverend Donald MacQueen, the minister of the parish at the time, went purposely to Trodda to check that gross superstition. He might have succeeded for a time in doing so, but it is known that many believed in the gruagach's existence long after that reverend gentleman's death."

The Gruagach of Arran Island

Another account of the gruagach or grogoch was given in 1895; it comes from West Bennan, on Arran Island in the Firth of Clyde.

This particular creature reputedly lived in a place called Uamh na Gruagaich, or sometimes Uamh na Beiste ("the cave of the grogoch" or "the cave of the monster"). This being was certainly female, for she herded, milked, and tended the cattle of Bennan, which was a female task there. Indeed, so diligent was she that no spring loss, no death loss, no mishap or disease ever befell the herd, and the cattle were the healthiest and fattest in all the Isles. In the morning, just before first light, the grogoch could be heard tending the animals and singing a melodious song in a clear and beautiful voice. It is said that she would wait on a hillock until the cattle were left for her supervision, but if any human approached her, she would disappear in the twinkling of an eye. If anyone attempted to capture her, it would be the worse for him or her.

The writer and folklorist Otta Swire, in *The Outer Hebrides and Their Legends* (1966), states:

"In old Gaelic, the word *gruagach* meant 'young chief,' or more literally 'long-haired one.' Later it came to be used of a spirit and in some districts (in Skye), a long-haired youth in a fine white shirt (often frilled) and knee-breeches; but more frequently in Skye, the gruagach was a very tall, thin woman with her hair falling to her feet. She wore a soft, misty robe, the effect being described as like a 'white reflection or shade.' She was usually the former mistress of the house or land she haunted, who had either died in childbirth or been put under enchantment. She belonged to the site and not to the occupant, and she was seldom seen unless something was about to happen at that site. She helped the owners by caring for cattle and small children (so long as they allowed no dog near her), and the simple were also under her protection. Like the English brownie, she was partial to a dish of cream. She could sometimes be seen weeping or showing great joy."

The Glaistig and the Vanathee

Many of the characteristics of the grogoch also apply to the glaistig—another female leprechaun-like creature in the Western Highlands. Like the grogoch, she lives in remote and isolated places—caves, old ruins, gullies, and abandoned houses—and largely shuns mortals whenever she can. There are few descriptions of her, but she is described as an untidy and dirty creature (like her male equivalent), with green hair and long yellow teeth. However, she is quite harmless and will do a good turn if called upon to do so.

In Ireland, there exists a solitary, female leprechaun-like creature known as the *vanathee* (from the Irish *bean an tí*—meaning "woman of the house"). This is a small, diligent woman—very much like the grogoch, but much tidier and more ordered—who will do tasks about the house to help the family to whom she attaches herself. She is, however, rather capricious and fickle in her ways, and will often attach herself to those who do not really deserve her attentions—the lazy and the slovenly—while ignoring those who would clearly benefit from her help. A libation of milk or cream should be left for her by the hearthside, and on no account must any attempt be made to see her as she performs her duties or collects her reward; otherwise, she will abandon the family and not return. Descriptions of her vary, but she is usually regarded as extremely small, dressed in a green skirt and white blouse, with a small cap on her head. It has also been suggested that she is rather ugly, and this may link her to the leprechaun.

Like the male grogoch, the vanathee is sometimes more of a hindrance than a help—although it has to be said that such instances are not very frequent. Occasionally, however, she will break or crack plates, move things around so they can't be found, or accidentally spill things in closed cupboards. In fact, she is often used as an explanation for all the little "accidents" that happen around the house.

In Ireland, vanathees are widely scattered across the country; in Brittany they are much more common, albeit in a slightly different form. Here, such female sprites attach themselves to houses rather than to families, and will usually aid the particular family that lives in a dwelling, even though this family may change from time to time. If the house is abandoned, the fairy continues to live there in ever greater isolation, even if the dwelling should crumble around her.

La Fée de Lanascol

The most famous of all such solitary female fairies is *La Fée de Lanascol*—a leprechaun-like sprite who inhabited the ruined château of Lanascol in rural Lower Brittany and who was famous throughout France. Although the château no longer stands, it was at one time a ruin, badly overgrown and falling in on itself. The name of the important local family who owned it has been all but forgotten in the district, but in the past a fairy made the derelict place very much her home, in the style of the Irish leprechaun.

The manor house at Lanascol must at one time have been an extremely important building, boasting extensive grounds crisscrossed by splendid avenues and walkways, with a grand and sweeping driveway leading up to it. Much of this is now gone, vanished beneath a carpet of leaves and advancing grasses. By the nineteenth century, the house itself had all but disappeared under wild creepers and vines. But the fairy was known to be still there. Many people claimed to have seen her, sweeping leaves and moss from the once grand driveway or working at an overgrown bush on the once well-tended lawns.

Her Appearance

Descriptions of her vary, for her clothing appears to differ from season to season, blending with her surroundings—if it is autumn, for example, she wears dull russet hues; if it is spring, she wears vibrant, green-tinged clothing. Sometimes she appears leaning on a crutch, in the form of an old and decrepit hag; sometimes she trips along the weedy walkways in the guise of a young maiden. At other times, she seems to be a grand lady who advances amid the overgrown parkland with an extremely stately bearing (in this guise she is often said to be followed by several small and utterly silent men, all dressed completely in black). As she passes, the ancient copper beeches that still line the driveway bow down as if to a queen, and the water trembles at her gaze.

The villagers—many of whom are farmers and laborers—all fear meeting her, for she can be regarded as a bad omen. If seen, she must not be approached, they warn. They refer to her as the *"groac'h Lanascol,"* or sometimes simply as "the lady."

In former times, she was said to be the guardian of a fabulous treasure hidden somewhere in the vicinity of the fallen château many years ago. This, of course, gives her the same status as the Irish leprechaun, who is also said to guard immeasurable wealth from former times. Indeed, it is said that the *fée* was so wealthy that when the Lanascol estate was put up for auction by the public notary at Plouaret, it was the fairy herself who bought the château and its grounds, and she is said to have remained their owner ever since.

More Leprechauns of Brittany and Scotland

This fairy is not unique in Breton folklore; there are many tales from all over Brittany of solitary female fairies living in ruined châteaux or manor houses. Professor Anatole le Braz, author of such works as *La Légende de la Mort* and *Au Pays des Pardons*, states that "Brittany has always been a kingdom of Fairie. One cannot even travel a league without brushing past the habitation of some male or female fairy." Many of these dwellings resemble the leprechaun's, and many Breton fées can be seen almost as "female leprechauns."

While not even the fairy of Lanascol, eerie though she is, is regarded as wholly evil, the same cannot be said for her sisters in Kintail, Scotland. Here, there is also a tradition of female fairies living alone in inaccessible places, but these are to be avoided at all costs. They are eaters of human flesh and drinkers of human blood. Although they resemble the traditional leprechaun in that they are (in their original form) naturally ugly and unkempt, they are also dangerous shape-shifters who can take on any form. However, they have cloven feet like a goat's, a telltale sign they cannot disguise. Their prey are the shepherds and cowherds who come to the remote places where they dwell to keep watch over their flocks or herds.

A story from Kintail records how the fairy uses her evil wiles against mortals.

PART I: WHO ARE THE LITTLE PEOPLE?

"The Fairy of Kintail"

Three men were hunting among the hills of Kintail. They had hunted all day, and as night came on, they took shelter in an old shieling ("hut") that was used by the shepherds of that area. They lit a fire, cooked some meat that they'd caught, and generally made themselves comfortable on some dry grass and moss. Two of them sat on one side of the fire while the third, on the other side, played a trump ("Jew's harp").

One of the pair began to talk of the day's hunting, of how long they'd been away from home and how he wished that he had his sweetheart with him. The other one expressed a similar sentiment. Now this was a foolish thing to do, since it is widely believed in Kintail that it is imprudent to wish for anything at night without first invoking the protection of the Deity, and this neither man had done.

Almost at once, the door of the shieling opened and a woman entered. The fire had burned down by now and threw out only a faint light, so none of the men could see very well, but each of the pair was sure that it was his sweetheart come to see him. Each thought he saw a different woman, you see. She sat down between them and put her arms affectionately around them, cuddling up to each one in turn.

The musician sat on the other side of the dim fire, watching this going on. Then, to his horror, he saw a thin stream of blood trickling toward him across the hearthstones. At the same time, he was able to see that the woman had the feet of a deer or a goat, and he knew immediately that this was a solitary fairy who lived in the high hills of Kintail and attacked travelers and wayfarers through her domain. The others could not see the danger—all each man saw was his own sweetheart.

In terror, the musician started up and dashed out of the hut. The fairy, realizing that she had been discovered, leaped up after him and pursued him from the place, galloping after him like the wind. He ran as fast as he could, and it was only thanks to his considerable physical fitness that he was able to outdistance her.

At last he reached the doorway of the nearest human habitation, and at this the fairy ceased her pursuit. He was brought in, white and trembling, and had to be revived by good mountain spirits before he could even tell what had happened.

The next morning the musician, together with some other men and a priest, went back to the shieling in the hills, where they found the badly mangled bodies of his two companions. Both of them had been drained of all their blood. Of the evil lone fairy, there was no sign, but every man there (including the priest) had the distinct impression that she was somewhere close by, maybe even watching them. That's the way of it with her kind.

Such blood-drinking female leprechaun-like creatures were also reported in some old folktales from Kerry (particularly in Macgillicuddy's Reeks and in the parish of Sneem). These were foul sprites who chiefly attacked those who refused to abide by the Black Fast during Lent (when even milk products were forbidden by the Church, and so tea was "black"), or who were morally lax in other ways. Sean O'Sullivan (himself a Kerryman), the famous archivist of the Irish Folklore Commission during the 1950s and 1960s, claimed to know of a fortress in the Reeks where these creatures resided. He mentioned this during a lecture in 1961, but it was never followed up, and the location of the place appears to have been lost. Perhaps this is just as well.

Although there appear to be no female leprechauns in the strictest sense of the term, there are a number of feminine sprites and fairies who, by virtue of their rather solitary condition and of their functions, seem to be related—albeit sometimes obliquely—to the leprechaun world. If there are any females of the pure leprechaun classification, they keep themselves extremely well hidden.

CHAPTER 6

How Long Do Leprechauns Live?

Although no reliable way to test the age of a leprechaun has yet been found, there is no doubt that each individual is incredibly old. It is said that the youngest of them can vividly remember "the days of Noll Cromwell in Ireland" (the 1650s), while the oldest of them state that they were here when the first Celts arrived (about 250 B.C.E.). Some folklorists have attributed this to so much blarney on the part of the leprechauns, but there may be at least some truth in these claims.

In order to find out anything about the age of a leprechaun, it is necessary to trick him into revealing it. This is not as easy as it may sound, for leprechauns—expert tricksters themselves—are not easily fooled. It is not enough to say, for example, "I'm sure that you remember such-and-such great event long past"; the leprechaun will sense what you are about, and feed you inaccurate information concerning the event. This will, in the end, cause you to doubt whether the leprechaun was there or not.

Tricking a Leprechaun

A favorite trick of those who want to know the true age of a leprechaun is, therefore, to reverse the process and give the leprechaun inaccurate information. Many leprechauns are full of their own importance as far as historical matters are concerned, and regard humans as rather stupid beings with no knowledge of history whatsoever. Therefore, one might, for instance, engage the leprechaun in conversation thus: "Ah, that Noll Cromwell—wasn't he a great and fine man? Didn't he serve the Irish people well? I hear they're erecting a monument to him on O'Connell Street in Dublin for all his kindness and charitable works here."

At this, the leprechaun will become terribly indignant, because none of his tribe has a shred of regard for Oliver Cromwell.

CROMWELL'S BIBLE

There is an old legend that Cromwell, the Lord Protector of England, lured several leprechauns onto an open Bible, which he then slammed shut, trapping them inside the Holy Word forever. In parts of County Clare, this act of base treachery is ascribed to Edmund Ludlow, the Cromwellian officer who led the first troops into the Burren. However, the tale of "Cromwell's Bible" still remains a sore point with many leprechauns, and his name must be spoken judiciously in their presence.

In reply to this insult, the leprechaun will answer: "Sure, wasn't he the most black-hearted cur that ever set foot in Ireland? Sure, I well mind myself..."

And, in his rage, he will launch into a personal anecdote about Cromwellian times in Ireland to prove his point. By doing so, he will prove that he was alive during the period, and this may be used to gauge his approximate age. Of course, such calculations may be wildly inaccurate.

Brian Boru

By contrast, most Irish leprechauns practically idolize Brian Boru—the great High King of Ireland during the late tenth and early eleventh centuries—and every leprechaun will swear that he was at the Battle of Clontarf in 1014, when, according to their tradition, "great Brian drove the heathen Dane from the shores of Ireland." Most of these stories are greatly exaggerated, although there may be some evidence that leprechauns were around at the time. However, it is extremely unlikely that any of them were involved in the fighting or that any of them sat, as their tradition states, "on Brian's shoulder so they could offer him advice."

The Viking Kings

Several leprechauns claim connections with other ancient kings. In fact, some claim association with the very Viking kings whom Brian and his forces drove out of Ireland. According to some traditions in Meath, for instance, at the Beltane Fair of 1898, a leprechaun by the name of Michael O'Reirdon, from County Wicklow, stated that he had been the chief advisor to King Ivarr II, Norse king of Dublin, prior to his defeat by the Dalriadic clans of Argyll in C.E. 914. O'Reirdon then went on to allege that it was because Ivarr paid no heed to the advice the leprechaun had given him that he was defeated in Scotland. (It should be remembered, however, that before making his assertions, O'Reirdon had consumed a vast quantity of poteen.) Several other leprechauns have claimed more tenuous links with Viking kings in both Limerick and Cork. It is through these connections that leprechauns have learned the locations of Viking treasure hoards, which propelled them to their position as the bankers of the fairy world.

Some leprechauns claim to be even older, stating that they can remember Irish kings before the time of recorded history. Many claim to have known Niall of the Nine Hostages—one of the great High Kings of Ireland, who led a number of successful expeditions into other parts of the ancient world—although their descriptions of the man and his temperament vary greatly. Some describe him as a great and powerful warrior of a "kindly disposition," while others claim he was "a smallish man with a bad and surly temper on him." Incidentally, conflicting accounts and descriptions of Brian Boru (whom many leprechauns claim to have known personally) are also given. He is described as a "young and fearless warrior, galloping into battle at the head of his troops against the Danish foe." At the time of Clontarf, Brian was seventy-two, and although he was killed by a Manx warrior (a soldier from the Isle of Man), he took no real part in the fighting.

Through their association with these ancient Irish kings, leprechauns also have access to the buried gold and jewels—hidden during wars and plagues—that are left over from those times. In fact, it is said that the laughremen of South Armagh guard a fabulous treasure that is supposed to lie near Emhain Macha (Navan Fort), the seat of the ancient kings of Ulster and some High Kings of Ireland.

The Tolcarne Troll

Across the Celtic world, some leprechauns claim even greater longevity. The town of Newlyn in Cornwall boasts a solitary being known as "the Tolcarne Troll" (although the use of the description "troll" may be inaccurate). He is described as "a little pleasant-looking old man" in a tight leather jerkin, with a great hood or cowl over his head. He is untidy and easygoing in his ways (and in this, he roughly corresponds to the representation of the leprechaun). Generally invisible, he makes his presence known by tiny sounds and grunts at the place where he lives—an odd outcropping of greenstone known as Newlyn Tolcarne, which was used by the druids for their rites in times long past.

This little gentleman claims he was alive in early biblical times and originally came from what is now the Holy Land. In fact, he says he came to Cornwall on a Phoenician ship trading for tin. He claims he spent his early years on various vessels sailing between Tyre (a large Phoenician city at the time) and the coasts of Cornwall and Ireland. After falling out with one of the captains, he was abandoned on the coast near Newlyn, where he waited for a Phoenician boat to return and take him home. None came, and he was allegedly forced to remain where he was.

Many stories have grown up around him—the chief one being that he acted as an oracle to Hiram, King of Tyre (in Lebanon), and that he assisted in the building of Solomon's holy temple in Israel. (Hiram and Solomon were contemporaries, and according to the Bible, Hiram did in fact supply cedars from his estates in Lebanon for the construction of Solomon's Temple.) In some variations of his story, however, the troll is described as "Odin the Wanderer" or simply as "the Wanderer," which connects him with the religion and folklore of the Vikings. He was also supposed to guard an enchanted glass known as the Mirror of the Ages, which could show the past, present, and future. Anyone could look into this mirror, provided he gave the little creature a tot of dark rum. Through the glass, people could behold what their ancestors had done in previous times, although they might not like what they saw.

Older Than the Pyramids

As to the troll's age, it was said he was old even when the pyramids were raised. Other fairies in Cornwall claim to remember the destruction of Sodom and Gomorrah, and some can even

CHAPTER 6: HOW LONG DO LEPRECHAUNS LIVE?

recall Noah's flood. In Cornwall, such assertions may well be taken as the truth, but in Ireland, where the leprechauns are full of blather, blarney, and poteen, they should be treated with grave suspicion.

Because of the exaggerations and outright lies of the Irish fairies, the true age of a leprechaun is very difficult to ascertain. As with all questions to a leprechaun, the investigator will probably never receive a satisfactory answer and will be forced to rely on guesswork. Leprechauns like to cultivate an air of mystery—and what better subjects for this than their origins and ages? All we can say with certainty is that they are all probably very old. However, the record for longevity probably belongs to an aged-looking grogoch in North Antrim. When asked what age he might be, he replied, "I have existed since the foundation of the world." Now that's old!

PART II

WHAT DO LEPRECHAUNS DO?

CHAPTER 7

SHOEMAKERS, BUILDERS, AND BLACKSMITHS

Traditionally, the most common profession for the leprechaun is that of fairy shoemaker. He is said to prepare and mend shoes for the Macara Shee (the trooping fairies), so that they can go on their travels through the countryside and attend grand balls and céilís within the fairy mounds and raths. Some accounts portray him as a shoemaker, actually preparing new shoes for the fairy balls, while others state that he is a shoe-repairer or cobbler, simply restoring those shoes which have been worn out by the unending dancing and frivolity.

Perhaps this distinction comes from a time when shoes and boots were expensive and much-prized items of clothing. About a century ago, many rural people still generally went about in bare feet and only wore shoes from time to time—if they owned a pair at all! Old local tales contain accounts of country children going to school in towns like Limerick and Waterford with their shoes hung around their necks, only putting them on when they reached the town limits. In Coleraine, in North Derry, there is a spot formerly known as the Barefoot Burn, where the country children washed their feet before putting on their boots to enter the town. Even as recently as the middle of the nineteenth century, most people in Ireland owned only one pair of boots, which lasted them the greater part of their lives. Traveling shoe-menders who went from one place to another were welcomed into communities and were counted as extremely important people, since they were the only ones with sufficient know-how to repair shoes and boots.

Shoemakers

The leprechaun, by association with these artisans, became a central figure in the fairy world. Fairies loved dancing and were always engaged in some ball or céilí, which often left their shoes in need of serious repair. Perhaps this is the origin of the word *leprechaun*, which, as we have already noted, may come from the ancient Irish *leith bhrógán* ("half-shoe–maker"): he repaired one shoe, half of a pair—the most worn shoe that the fairy had ruined with his or her dancing.

In many tales concerning leprechauns, the creature gives away his position in drains and ditches by the tapping of his tiny hammer as he works on a shoe or boot. He is to be seen with his last and waxed strings, sitting cross-legged (in the fashion of country tailors and shoe-menders) in the shade of a bush or the stump of a tree, or in the dry part of some gully. If he is so absorbed, then it is worthwhile to make a sudden grab for him, to see if he can be caught.

However, shoemaking is not the only form of employment in which the leprechaun can be engaged. There are numerous stories which speak of leprechauns undertaking other forms of work, for the sprite is nothing if not highly industrious and enterprising in his choice of occupations.

Leprechauns As Builders

It is thought that the earliest forms of leprechauns or leprechaun-like fairies were not shoe-menders at all, but rather builders and stonemasons. This theory probably has its origins in the number of tiny piles or hummocks of stones to be found in fields and moors throughout the Celtic countryside. In Ireland, these were known as *leachts*, and were said to mark the spots where victims had died during the Great Famine of 1845–52. There may, however, be an older explanation, for these stone piles clearly existed long before the nineteenth century. It is said that they once marked the sites of leprechauns' houses, and that they were erected by the wee folk as signals that no one else could build there.

In some areas of the Celtic world, leprechaun-like people were credited with building the mounds and tumuli in which the Tuatha dé Danann came to dwell. They may also have been associated with tiny settlements of stone houses to be found in the Orkneys (Skara Brae) and on the northern islands of Sanday and Westray, since these buildings are very small. Old stories around such places speak of tiny groups of builders—a small, wizened people from the north—who built their communities in extremely isolated and inhospitable places, mainly on islands. The bulk of these houses were underground, to protect them from the fierce winds and sand that blew across these places in the winter months. The tiny people were said to be skilled at building and stonemasonry, but they kept themselves (and their secrets) to themselves, preferring to stay well away from other islanders. They were farmers, keeping cattle and carving out small cultivated areas for themselves, but they were also sometimes counted as supernatural beings with strange and magical ways. They seem to have vanished just as mysteriously as they came, leaving only their houses behind them. Because they lived mostly underground, later peoples saw them as fairies, brownies or leprechaun-like beings.

The notion that leprechauns might live underground was once widespread in several parts of Ireland—for example, Cork, Limerick, Clare, and Westmeath. On the islands off the Irish coast, too, they built underground shelters for themselves and for other fairies.

"Houses and Potatoes"

For mortal people, living side-by-side with such builders was not always easy. An old tale from Rathlin Island in North Antrim speaks of fairies who decided to build a new house close to a human settlement:

There was a man on Rathlin called Tommy Anderson, one time, and he had the notion of building a new house. It was not for himself, you

CHAPTER 7: SHOEMAKERS, BUILDERS, AND BLACKSMITHS

understand, but for his mother, who'd become very old and infirm. Her name was Peggy Bradley and she was a widow and couldn't get about all that much. He thought that they could all live together in the one house, and that he and his wife could look after her. He built a place up at Cabbal, near the West Lighthouse—a right tidy place it was—and lived there snug enough for a while.

One evening they were all draining potatoes by the door, and the water was running everywhere. There was a sharp and angry knock on the door, and when Tommy went to see what it was, there was a wee runt of a man in a skirty coat waiting for him. He was an ugly wee fellow, all burned with the sun and wearing a pair of oul' brogues on him that no tinker would wear. And he had a pipe rammed in the corner of his mouth like a sailor.

Tommy knew that this was one of the Thane-a-korr (the local name for a leprechaun-like creature), and he asked him what he wanted.

The little man said that he had been building houses for the fairy people in that particular area, and that the potato water was causing everybody great distress. He also told Tommy that this place was now a fairy place, and that he and his family would have to move on and let the little man build more fairy houses (which were underground, if you understand). If he didn't, the Thane-a-korr would take their vengeance and would make life very miserable for himself and his old mother. In the meantime, he was to stop teeming potatoes by the cottage doorway.

And with that, the little man turned and was gone without a by-your-leave.

Tommy took it all very seriously, for he didn't want to get on the wrong side of the fairy builders, and so he moved all his family to another part of the island, and the grand, tidy house that he'd built was eventually pulled down.

There are people that will tell you that there's still fairy building going on up at Cabbal yet. It's a fairy place, all right. Not even the lighthouse-men would go near it.

Underground Houses

Leprechauns often built underground fairy dwellings wherever they wished, and this could be difficult for humans living in the vicinity. Some of the most favored constructions were "céilí-houses"—places where fairies would gather to make merry. This could often lead to excessive noise and clamor, particularly at night when humans were trying to sleep. There was really nothing that they could do; like Tommy Anderson in the previous story, they would have to move elsewhere. The best they could hope for was that no leprechauns would choose to build dwellings within their immediate vicinity.

Leprechauns As Metalworkers and Smiths

In some respects, leprechauns share certain work-related characteristics with the goblins of Germany and Switzerland. These little fellows are often described as both miners and metalworkers, and are skilled in forging iron and copper. In parts of Ireland and Scotland, too, leprechauns and brownies are sometimes described as tinkers and metal-beaters rather than as shoe-menders or cobblers. The tapping that humans sometimes hear is not always the sound of the sprite working on a brogue or a shoe; sometimes it is the noise of him repairing an old pot or pan, or shaping a bit of pliable metal.

Although some leprechauns are particularly skilled in metalwork—examples of their work are often seen at the fairy fairs and goblin markets which are to be found in remote areas of the Celtic countries—the majority of them are not. They can temporarily patch up broken implements, but this is really the extent of their expertise. This lack of specialized skill, however, does not prevent them from setting up as skilled tinsmiths, even though the work that they produce is quite often substandard and shoddy. Nor does it prevent them from claiming great skills—many will assert, for example, that they have been metalworkers and even goldsmiths to the great High Kings of Ulster, especially Brian Boru and Niall of the Nine Hostages.

Blacksmiths

Leprechauns—particularly the larger varieties—sometimes also claim some skill as blacksmiths. In many rural areas, blacksmiths also served as metalworkers, making kettles, pots, and pans for the people, and this fits in well with the leprechaun's exaggerated claims of skill in that area.

It is quite probable that most of these sprites have been nowhere near an ordinary horse, because most animals show a particular aversion to the fairy kind; nevertheless, the leprechaun may declare himself to be a master blacksmith who will only work with "horses of the fairy kind."

The leprechaun does not operate his own forge, as a blacksmith might in the human world. Rather, he takes over an old forge that has been abandoned or allowed to fall into ruin and neglect, and uses it for his own purposes. It is said that the ghosts of the dead often congregate at such places, and leprechauns appear to have the power to commandeer these spirits into helping them in their "work." The ghosts of the dead—particularly those who had died suddenly, perhaps in some accident—were especially vulnerable to leprechaun influence.

FAIRY HORSES

Fairy horses are not horses as we mortals understand them. Rather, they have the appearance of horses, but are really old sticks, brooms, or fence pieces that have been transformed into the likeness of horses through fairy glamour. By pretending to shoe these creatures, the leprechaun perpetuates the illusion and so deceives those who are watching him.

CHAPTER 8

MUSICIANS, MUSIC, AND FESTIVALS

Like all fairies, leprechauns have a great love of music and are often skilled musicians. Because leprechauns have such phenomenal memories, they can carry tunes in their heads long after mortals have forgotten them. As a result, leprechauns can both remember and play—note for note—ancient folk tunes that are no longer available to most mortal musicians. Many a fiddler or pipe player, and many a harpist too, has heard strange and beautiful melodies wafting on the morning or evening breeze from bogs and hollows where leprechauns are said to dwell. Rory Dall O'Cahan, the composer credited with one of the most famous of all Irish melodies—"The Londonderry Air," better known as "Danny Boy"—reportedly heard it being played upon a leprechaun's harp along the marshy banks of the River Roe in North Derry. He wrote it down, and its beauty has entranced Irish people (and many others) ever since. It is said to be one of the very few tunes that can reduce a true Irishman to tears when he hears it.

THE CELTIC HARP
The Celtic harp is a typical leprechaun instrument. Found in both Ireland and Scotland, it dates to at least the twelfth century; the traveler and writer Gerald of Wales (c. 1146–c. 1223) mentions them in a book about Ireland. The strings are metal, which gives them a great resonance.

"Don't Copy Leprechaun Music"

Because of the great beauty and antiquity of their melodies, leprechauns are said to guard them strictly. Woe to the musician who writes down a fairy tune and passes it off as his own, for the "wee people" will be sure to have their revenge upon such an upstart! An old and frequently repeated tale from the west of Ireland illustrates this point:

There was a piper in Mayo one time—one of the O'Malleys—who was very much in demand for the skill of his playing and the sweetness of his tunes. He lived in a little house near the coast, with only his dog for company, for he was a solitary man who preferred his own company most of the time.

One evening, he had been playing at a céilí in Castlebar and the festivities had gone on throughout the night. So it was early in the morning that he was making his way home. He had only gone a couple of miles from the céilí-house when he chanced on a little glen close by the roadside. I won't tell you where it is, for it is a fairy place and the leprechauns can often be seen there yet, gambolling and sporting, even at midday.

Well, as the piper O'Malley passed by this glen, he heard music drifting up into the morning air from the hollow below. He ventured down to take a closer look, his little dog slinking down through the bushes behind him. A leprechaun was sitting on a large rock in the middle of a stream, playing on a set of ancient pipes, and the melody he played was so beautiful that it would have broken your heart to hear it.

The Music Remembered

Now, O'Malley had a great ear for the notes and a great memory for the music, and he was able to remember the tune as it floated around him on the breeze. He stole back to the road and made his way home, keeping the music in his head all the while.

From that day onward, he included the fairy tune among those he played, and he always passed it off as his own. He never told anyone he'd heard it from a leprechaun. Everyone who heard it thought it was a most beautiful melody and declared that O'Malley was little short of a genius for having composed (as they thought) such a delicate air. But fairy tunes are not to be trifled with or to be claimed by mortals as their own.

Some time after, O'Malley was playing at a céilí on the wild Mayo coast. He played the fairy air several times, and the people were well satisfied. Again, it was early in the morning when he set out for home, with his dog at his heels. As they were passing through a particularly remote part of the coast, O'Malley suddenly heard yet another tune being played on the pipes, even more beautiful than the first he'd heard. He made his way down to see who was playing, with his dog close behind him.

The Music in the Cave

The music seemed to be coming from a large cave in the cliff face a little way below him. He looked around for a way down, and sure enough, there was a little gravel path leading down to the very mouth of the cavern. Without hesitating, the piper O'Malley scrambled down, his mouth fairly watering at the thought of stealing another melody from the fairies.

However, as he stood at the mouth of the cave, the music suddenly seemed less distinct and farther away. To hear it better, the piper stepped into the cave, going farther and farther into its depths. His dog followed close at his heels.

That was the last anyone saw of the piper O'Malley, although his dog did appear some time later, shaking with fear, out of a burrow two or three miles away. But no trace of his master has been found, even to this day.

Still, if you should venture along the Mayo coastline at certain times of the year, and if you should happen to be passing a place where there are caves, you may hear the strains of music coming from the depths of one of them. It is a lonely, eerie sound, and so beautiful it will break your heart to hear it. People will tell you that it is the music of the piper O'Malley, held as a prisoner in the Otherworld by the leprechauns whose tune he stole, and that the music contains the strains of his longing to get back to the mortal realm. Of course, there are those who will tell you that there is nothing to it—that it is only the sound of the wind in the caves—but I'll wager that there are few of them who will venture deep into these caverns to investigate. And these same people will stay well away from the rugged and lonely Mayo coastline at certain times of the year. That's the vengeance of the leprechauns, all right—for they disapprove very strongly of people taking their tunes and claiming them for their own. That's the way of it, all right.

Skill at Music

As the previous story demonstrates, leprechauns are very skilled musicians who can turn their hands to any tune. This skill, they claim, has been handed down to all fairy kind since the days of the Tuatha dé Danann, who came from the east (or the sun, depending on the version of the tale) in a golden mist and brought music, poetry, and culture to Ireland. The Tuatha dé Danann also brought the Irish harp, the simplest-seeming of all musical instruments and yet one of the hardest to play. The Gaels took over the playing of the harp and used it at great banquets and feasts, and the leprechauns mimic this ability and will sometimes play the harp at their own gatherings. However, while they can turn their hands to almost any instrument, they greatly favor the fiddle or the Irish pipes.

Many of the old songs and tunes which they play are said to come from the earliest times—from the period of the Tuatha dé Danann themselves. This is not always true, for leprechauns remember old mortal melodies people have long forgotten and can often play them note for note, passing them off as mystical fairy tunes. The music of the Tuatha dé Danann is more abstract than this; it is quite ethereal and is not really suited to any human instrument except the harp.

Magic in the Music

One must always be extremely careful when listening to leprechaun music, especially the livelier jigs and reels. The sprite may include some magic within the tune, and—like the girl in the story told in an earlier chapter—the listener may find it impossible to resist dancing. Seeing that he has the dancer in his power, the leprechaun will increase the speed and tempo of the tune, making his captive leap and gambol faster and faster in time with the music. This he does for spite and mischief, and some people have been known to die from exhaustion after performing a "leprechaun's reel."

MUNSTER MUSICIANS

The greatest leprechaun harpers and pipers are generally said to come from the Munster area, while the best of the fiddle-players and lyricists are believed to reside in Ulster. It is said that leprechaun tunes have no lyrics until they drift into Ulster, and that their poems have no melody until they come farther south. This, of course, is not strictly true, but it serves as a rule of thumb.

To exchange melodies, poems, and lyrics, leprechauns from all over Ireland meet at gatherings and fairs that take place at certain times of the year. Here, they play one another the latest melodies they have acquired, and in this way the tunes pass into the general fairy repertoire.

Festivals and Céilís

There is nothing the leprechaun likes more than a good céilí, since these are nothing more than excuses for intemperate drinking and merrymaking. Because of his solitary nature, he does not get the opportunity for either very often, so he has to make the most of such gatherings when and as they come along.

There are, however, a number of fixed dates in the leprechaun's social calendar.

May Eve and Halloween

The two most important gatherings are at May Eve and at Halloween. These are, of course, general fairy festivals, when the gates of the raths and mounds of the Sídhe are thrown open and the Macara Shee (the fairy cavalcade) takes to the road on its progress through the countryside. These festivals divide the year into two halves—light and dark, warm and cool—and provide opportunities for the fairies to show their finery. The leprechaun, having no such finery to show, turns his hand to other things; it is usually at these times of the year that he moves house (if he has a mind to) or makes repairs to his dwelling. These festivals are also opportunities for him to erect new stills for his illegal spirits, or to seek out new places where such stills can be situated.

May Eve (April 30–May 1)

This marks the start of the summer, which is a celebration of the return to strength and optimism regarding growing things and new life. The festival also looks forward to the year's harvest, and so it had great significance for our ancient agricultural ancestors. It is at this time that the leprechaun makes the most of his illicit spirits, which he stores away for the coming year at various locations scattered across the countryside. There are gatherings in various parts of the country, as leprechauns arrive to sample one another's batches of poteen, and the mood is incredibly drunken and lively.

WALPURGIS NIGHT

May Eve is also celebrated in Europe as Walpurgis Night, a celebration of Saint Walpurga. In some areas of Germany and Eastern Europe, it is also believed that on Walpurgis Night, witches' covens meet and evil spirits hold sway.

Halloween (October 31)

This, on the other hand, is a gloomy and somber time, when one's thoughts are reflective and focused on the year that is almost past. Once again, the Macara Shee troop around the countryside, but this time there is an added element to their cavalcade. This is the time when the veil between the mortal world and the Otherworld is at its most fragile, and many unsettling creatures can cross from the Beyond into our own world to walk abroad. It is the time when the banshee utters her wailing cry, signifying death in the year to come; and the pooka gallops along ill-lit lanes, terrifying animals, curdling the milk in the udders of cows, and preventing hens from laying. It is also a time when the shrouded, unquiet dead roam the highways and byways of the land.

THE POOKA

The pooka (also spelled *púca*) is a Celtic spirit. It's similar to the leprechaun in that it can be both good and mischief-making. As a shape-shifter, it takes many forms. It even entered American popular culture; in the 1950 film *Harvey*, starring Jimmy Stewart and Josephine Hull, Stewart's best friend is an invisible six-foot-tall rabbit named Harvey. Stewart makes clear that Harvey is a pooka who adopted him as his friend.

The leprechaun is not greatly bothered by the banshee or the pooka, or even by the wandering ghosts; he simply keeps out of their way. Besides, he has a number of tricks of his own to play. It is at this time of year that he is at his most mischievous, and he celebrates the fact by turning the farmer's livestock out of the fields and onto the road; by taking farm gates off their hinges; by causing drafts in chimneys, so smoke blows down into the kitchen; and by a hundred other pranks. Sometimes at Halloween, leprechauns will gather together (although not in such great numbers as at May Eve) to play their pranks and will become very intoxicated, thus adding to their mischief. Small feasts, composed of hazelnuts, apples, and fairy butter, are consumed at such revelries, and locally distilled poteen, suitably aged, is drunk with some gusto.

Saint Brigid's Day (February 1)

Besides these two great festivals (which are, of course, as important to mortals as they are to the fairy folk), there are other times during the year when the leprechauns will come together to make merry. One of the most important is Saint Brigid's Day.

Although Brigid is the foremost female Christian saint in Ireland, tradition tells us that before her conversion she was a *draoi-ban* (a female druid or pagan priestess) and was always a friend to the Little People. Besides, the date of her celebration coincides with the end of winter, the lengthening of the days and the promise of longer evenings; it became known to the Church as Candlemas (the onset of longer evenings is reflected in the old maxim, "On Candlemas Day throw a candle away"). Before Christianity took it over, however, this was celebrated as a pagan festival, and so the leprechauns (who can well remember the ancient festival) will make merry in celebration of the increased daylight and the formerly pagan saint.

PART II: WHAT DO LEPRECHAUNS DO?

> **THE GODDESS BRIGHID**
> The ancient Celts worshiped the goddess Brighid, patroness of poetry and seership. She was a triple goddess, with three aspects, of which this was one. Another aspect looked after the forge, while another was the patroness of healing. It's not known if Saint Brigid really existed, but the stories about her took on many characteristics of the Celtic goddess.

Saint Patrick's Day and Other Holidays

Another time when leprechauns gather together is on Saint Patrick's Day (March 17). Although the patron saint of Ireland is not well-regarded among the fairy kind (he tricked them out of part of their lands by subtle argument), his feast was at one time celebrated by mortals the length and breadth of Ireland; much of the festivity involved strong liquor, and since large amounts of it tended to be spilled (in ceremonies such as "drowning the shamrock"), leprechauns took it as a time of festivity as well, catching all the food and drink that fell from human tables and claiming it for their own.

Lughnasadh

The ancient Celtic feast of Lughnasadh (July 31–August 1), also known as Lammas, is another festive date in the leprechaun's calendar, although a relatively minor one. Strictly speaking, this is a festival for witches—one of darkness and ill omen. In Kerry, the second week of August was at one time known as the festival of Lughnasa or Crom Dubh's Day (the dark Lugh festival); it signaled a turn toward darker days and a time when the forces of evil and cold might begin to flex their muscles once again. It was one of the great Sabbats of the witch's year and as such had little to do with the fairies. Nevertheless, leprechauns still observe it as a kind of minor festival, perhaps to prepare themselves for the dark days of winter or to signal the approaching end of summer. Festivities and merriment are kept to a minimum, and food for the feast consists mainly of old potatoes and kale or cabbage tops, washed down by the invariable plentiful supply of poteen.

Yule

Only one other feast day is observed by the sprites. This is the great festival of Yule (December 25). All living things, natural and supernatural, celebrate the turning of the year. During this time, the leprechaun must not touch liquor at all. In an act of defiance, many leprechauns spend the day counting their hoards of treasure and gold, in preparation for the coming year. As soon as Saint Stephen's Day (December 26) comes round, they are back to their pranks and drinking again.

Uisneach

There is one other festival which, although not a feast day, is specific to leprechauns. This is the Beltane Fair of Uisneach, held each year in County Westmeath just before May Day—usually around April 28 or 29. Leprechauns travel to this fair from all over Ireland. They come to exchange tunes, riddles, stories, and songs and to show off their prowess at brewing and distilling and at sports and music. This is also the arena where disputes can be settled and alliances made. Goods are sold at the fair—usually homemade foods, shoes, and articles stolen from humans.

> ### THE HILL OF UISNEACH
> In County Westmeath, there is a hill, the Hill of Uisneach, considered to be the symbolic center of Ireland. The fire to mark the start of Beltane was, it is said, set here in ancient times. It marked a place where the borders of Leinster, Munster, Connaught, Ulster, and Meath all met. Today various ancient artifacts can still be seen on the site.

The event usually runs for several days, culminating in the May Day celebrations. According to some accounts, however, in 1846 and 1847, the event had to be delayed because of the Irish Potato Famine and difficulties in traveling. On one famous occasion, in 1901, the celebrants became so intoxicated that the fair came to an end because no one was sober enough. Such instances, however, are extremely rare. A few mortals have been permitted to witness this occasion, but it is said those who do invariably forget everything they have seen within two or three days.

Although a solitary creature by nature, the leprechaun certainly knows how to party—and he will take every opportunity to do so. This means he will break into houses and drink from any container of strong liquor he may find. From time to time, he will become extremely noisy and boisterous. If approached in this condition, he will become extremely aggressive and abusive, so it is best to leave him alone. Although some folklorists argue that this is the best time to capture him—while he is drunk and inside a house—this might not be the case: the leprechaun's reflexes are still extremely quick, and the would-be captor may find he receives more than he bargained for.

CHAPTER 9

LEPRECHAUN ENTERTAINMENT

Reference has already been made to the leprechaun's great skill at (and love of) distilling spirits. In many ways, this reflects the traditions of the Irish peasantry many years ago. Nowadays, we tend to obtain our liquor from pubs or other establishments, but in days gone by this was not always the case. Distilling was once quite common in many parts of the country, and many cottages had their own stills. Most country people were able to distill at least some form of spirit—although whether it was actually drinkable or not is open to question. There were those, of course, who were very skilled in the distilling art and could produce spirits of superior quality.

The leprechaun was the most skilled distiller in the fairy world. The poteen he produced was the sweetest liquor ever tasted. However, few people seem to have tasted it, since the leprechaun consumes most of his own produce. Perhaps this is just as well; mortals should never accept drink from a leprechaun, as it will rob them of their senses and take away their memories.

Distillers to the Fairies

Leprechauns were supposed to provide all the spirits, wines, and ales consumed at fairy functions. These were prepared in such a way that, if the fairies were to invite mortals to join in their revelries, those who drank from the "fairy cup" would forget their homes, their wives and sweethearts, their children and property, and live among the fairies ever after, oblivious to the outside world. It was said that leprechaun poteen was like a drug to the senses of any mortal man or woman.

If fairies were to drink from the cup, however, they would become all the more merry and raucous, and would get up to all sorts of mischief and foolery. They would dance longer and livelier; they would roar and laugh and tell old stories and sing old songs. The leprechaun's liquor had the effect of making even the gloomiest fairies exceedingly jolly. Sometimes it also made them susceptible to the leprechaun's will, so each proffered draft had to be judged with care.

Leprechauns As Musicians

The leprechaun's abilities as a professional musician have also already been discussed. The leprechaun is a highly skilled musician who has a long memory and remembers old tunes that all mortals (and most fairies) have long forgotten. Indeed, the leprechaun's repertoire stretches back almost to the birth of Celtic music. It is said that the first leprechauns were great harpists, and that they taught the early bards of Ireland their skills and music. Nowadays, they are more at home with the fiddle or the Irish pipes, although a number of them are also known to be great bodhrán players.

Most of the tunes leprechauns play are so old that they have no titles, and those mortal musicians who sometimes "borrow" them have to give them names—"The Hare in the Barley," "Seamus McInanders" (both relatively well-known tunes, recorded from County Down leprechauns), and so on. Sometimes the stolen leprechaun music is simply given a general title, such as "The Music of the Ghosts"—a series of consecutive tunes heard and recaptured by a fisherman on Great Blasket Island, off the Kerry coast. Not that it is easy to steal a leprechaun's tune, for they take their music very seriously and guard their melodies with a fierce jealousy. Any mortal who does manage to steal a melody will usually find that some serious ill befalls him before too long, as the leprechaun takes his revenge.

THE BODHRÁN

The bodhrán is an Irish drum. It's one sided, making it a frame drum, and played either with the hand or with a wooden beater. Its origin is not clear; some say it dates from the middle of the nineteenth century, but others believe it is much more ancient. Whatever the case, it is an essential accompaniment to Irish music.

PART II: WHAT DO LEPRECHAUNS DO?

Leprechauns will usually play only at gatherings, and this is where most of their ancient tunes are to be heard. In order to hear a leprechaun play, one must go to a place where fairies are known to congregate—an old fort or rath, maybe, or simply a riverbank—late in the evening. This is when the "Good Folk" gather for a céilí, and one is bound to hear at least two or three old tunes. It is, however, advisable to be extremely careful; leprechaun music is known to have an intoxicating effect upon even the dourest mortals, making them leap and dance right away.

DANCING THE FEET AWAY

There is a famous story, recounted in areas ranging from North Antrim to Limerick, of a woman who overheard the leprechauns playing and danced so enthusiastically that she danced all her toes off!

Interspersed with the music are old stories and ballads sung in the *sean-nós* style (unaccompanied). Despite their rather ugly looks and bedraggled appearance, leprechauns have exceptionally fine singing voices. Indeed, it is said that many great opera stars would give anything to have the pitch and range of a leprechaun in full voice. "To hear one of them sing," observed an old Leitrim woman, "would make the tears start in your eyes."

Ghost Stories

Leprechauns are also well-versed in old stories, particularly in ghostly and humorous tales. Their memories are phenomenal, and their knowledge of antique Irish texts is unsurpassed. And it is well known that—their ungainly attributes aside—they are exceptionally fine dancers and can perform jigs and reels to perfection.

In spite of his surly looks, the leprechaun can be quite a cultivated fairy when he chooses to be—perhaps even more so than the rather fickle sprites who comprise the Macara Shee. It is little wonder, then, that he is very frequently sought as an entertainer at the fairy balls. However, his price for such services, like any other superstar's, is said to be very high. And it is to leprechauns and money that we must now turn.

CHAPTER 10

GUARDIANS OF GOLD

There is no doubt that leprechauns are the nearest thing the fairy world has to bank managers. In fact, some folklorists argue that this is their primary function, superseding all of their other occupations.

Leprechauns, it is said, have access to untold wealth. As has already been mentioned, they remember where all the ancient treasures are hidden, all across Ireland. These treasures include the wealth of long-dead Irish kings, the plunder of the Vikings who once raided the coasts, Norman gold and the pillaged booty of pirates. They also know, through supernatural means, where misers have hidden their hoards and where local aristocrats have concealed their money against robbery. These hoards add up to a total of millions of pounds, and their exact locations are locked away in each leprechaun's head.

Where Does He Keep It?

However, the leprechaun is something of a miser himself, and refuses to share this knowledge with any other fairy. Thus, each leprechaun is the guardian of all the secret wealth in Ireland (and perhaps even in other Celtic countries). So when the trooping fairies seek to dispense largesse, or to reward some mortal for some kindness he or she has performed toward them, it is to the leprechaun they must go for money. If, as is sometimes said, a bank manager has a heart of stone, then the heart of the leprechaun is even harder. Seldom does he part with any of the wealth, and he sits as self-appointed judge over the fickle (as he considers it) conduct of the other fairies.

Nor does he keep all this treasure anywhere near his home; it is sufficient for him to know its various locations. However, he will sometimes keep a fraction of it to hand, in order to cover any unexpected expenses that he may incur. The gold (for such it is) is usually kept in an old butter-crock, iron pot, or some similar container. This has led to the idea—commonly held among mortals—that each leprechaun possesses a crock of gold. It is also generally believed that he marks its location with a rainbow—so the crock lies at the end of a natural (or supernatural) phenomenon. All the treasure-hunter has to do, therefore, is follow the rainbow to its end (the place where it appears to touch the ground) in order to find the leprechaun's wealth. As with everything else about the leprechaun tribe, this is not as easy as it first appears; nobody has yet reached the rainbow's end to claim his or her fortune. Many people have spent fruitless days in chasing rainbows, eventually coming away with nothing at all.

Fairy Banker

In his role as fairy banker, each leprechaun carries with him two black leather pouches. In one there is a silver shilling—which magically returns to the purse every time it is paid out, so that the leprechaun can appear to pay out large sums of money without ever parting with a shilling. In the other pouch he carries a coin of gold—usually from an antique period—with which he will try to bribe his way out of tricky situations. However, those who accept this coin should beware: it will usually turn to leaves or ashes (its natural form) soon after the leprechaun has parted with it. Both these coins serve to confirm the fairy's tricky nature with regard to money.

> **LEPRECHAUN GOLD IN THE POTTERVERSE**
>
> Leprechaun gold makes a brief appearance in the Harry Potter universe when the affable rogue Ludo Bagman pays off gambling debts to the Weasley twins in what appears to be genuine gold coins. The coins, which are leprechaun gold, vanish in a few hours, leaving the twins furious at Bagman.

Tales concerning mortals who try to extract the treasure's whereabouts from a leprechaun are legion throughout Ireland. Leprechauns are naturally suspicious of humans, whom they believe to be rather stupid, inferior creatures, and so they delight in outwitting mortals who try to force them to reveal their hidden riches. If one should catch a leprechaun and demand to be taken to his nearest cache of wealth, one must never take one's eyes off him for a second, or he will disappear in a flash. Hold tight to him and keep concentrating on him until you reach the treasure. Even then, he will try many tricks to escape or to make the riches vanish.

"The Leprechaun and His Hoard"

A well-known story, told all over Ireland, illustrates the previous point. This particular version of it is from Kerry.

There was a man living near Listowel one time who had a blind sister and an old mother to look after. You can imagine that they were all very poor, and the man had sometimes hardly a rag of a shirt to put on his back.

One day, he was out cutting peats in the bog for the winter stacks. He was just cutting close to what looked like an old bush when he saw a sudden movement under the leaves. He stopped; the leaves rustled again, and out from underneath them came a little man, only a bit longer than a forefinger. He was an untidy-looking creature with a large, wide-brimmed hat and an old claw-hammer coat, black with dirt, across his back. Seeing the man cutting peats, he made a dart to the side and went to disappear into the heather that was growing on the surface of the bog.

But the man was quicker. Almost instinctively, he stuck out his foot and caught the end of the coat as the little man made to dart away. He knew right well that this was a leprechaun and that he had a crock of gold hidden somewhere nearby. If he could get his hands on those riches, his sister and his mother would never have to worry about anything again. And he would be one of the richest men in the county himself.

Bending down, he scooped the little man into the hollow of his hand before he could vanish into the thicket.

"Oh, murther!" screamed the leprechaun. "It's a bad day in Ireland, to be sure, when an honest tradesman can't go about his business without being set upon by rogues! Not since the days of Black Cromwell—bad cess to his name—was ever a poor and innocent traveler so harried!"

But the man just laughed. "There's nothing innocent about you, my little maneen," he exclaimed. "Now take me to your crock of gold!"

The leprechaun simply made a sound that was somewhere between a snort and a laugh, and spat onto the other's clenched fist. "Ah, I have no crock of gold!" he replied. "Sure, and I'm only a poor tradesman—where would I get all the money ye think that I might have? Now put me down, like a sensible fellow, and let me go about my own business!"

But the mortal shook his head. "Not until ye show me where yer crock of gold lies," he retorted.

The Leprechaun Surrenders

The leprechaun heaved a great sigh. "That's just an oul' story put about by mortals that know no better!" he insisted. "I thought that a decent fellow like yourself would have had more wit about you than to believe them. It's well known that leprechauns such as myself are as poor as church mice, and I'd wager that you've more money about you at this second than I've had in my whole long life, and that's a fact."

But the man was not to be turned. He tightened his fist, squeezing the leprechaun mercilessly. "Where is your crock of gold?" he repeated. "For I'm not setting you down till you tell me."

The leprechaun gasped and spluttered. "All right! All right! Stop yer squeezin'. It's true that I might have a little bit of money put by, but it's hardly worth botherin' about, and it would certainly be of no interest to a fine, well-heeled gentleman such as yerself."

But his captor was in no mood for his silver-tongued flattery. "I'll be the judge of that," he told the leprechaun. "Take me to it. Is it far from here?"

The leprechaun shook his head. "Not far," he said. "But a decent fellow like yerself wouldn't take away the last penny of an honest artisan, now would he?"

Without a word, the man tightened his grip.

"All right! I'll take you to it." And, hoisting himself up in the fellow's fist, he pointed out the road that they were to go.

Following the pointing finger, his captor walked all the way down a boreen and over a stile (never once lifting his eyes off the sprite, in case he should disappear) and across several fields. At last they came to a large stand of trees—too big to be called a copse and too small to be called a wood.

The Leprechaun Tricks the Mortal

"Here we are," said the leprechaun, pointing into its dark depths. "I've hidden my poor savings at the base of one of these trees. Now let me go and be about my own business."

But the other kept a tight grip on him. "Show me exactly where it is," he insisted, stepping in amongst the trees. The fairy had no other option but to remain where he was and guide his captor into the depths of the grove.

At length they stopped before a large tree which didn't look any different from any of the others around it. The leprechaun waved a hand in its general direction.

"There it is!" he almost shouted. "There's where my poor savings are hidden. And much good may they do ye. Now let me go, ye bullyin' robber!"

But the man shook his head. "How do I know that you're not playin' me for a fool?" he asked. "You could point to any oul' tree and tell me that there was wealth buried under it, and you'd be away, quick as a wink, before I'd find out yer lies."

The leprechaun waved a dismissive hand in the air. "Very well," he said in exasperation. "Was ever there so much distrust in the heart of a scoundrel since the days of Black Cromwell? Look at the foot of the tree, an' I'll show ye the fortune that is lying there."

The man looked, but all the same he kept one eye on the leprechaun in case he would disappear. And as he looked, he suddenly seemed to see through the ground, as if he was looking down into a pool of water; and in a hollow in the roots of the tree he saw several butter-crocks with gold coins spilling out of them, and strings of pearls and diamonds lying beside them. It was a great fortune, to be sure—far more than his blind sister and widowed mother would ever need for the rest of their lives. The sight of it almost took his breath away.

"There ye are!" said the leprechaun. "Would I try t'cheat ye? Now put me down and go and get something to dig it up with."

The man's eyes narrowed, for he suspected that the leprechaun might be tricking him. "And as soon as I set you down and go for a shovel, you'll move the treasure somewhere else," he said warily. "I know your sort, my little maneen."

The leprechaun merely snorted. "I'll do nothing of the sort," he said airily. "Indeed, you have my word that I won't lay a finger on it. Now set me down."

The man looked around him. Every tree in the grove was the same, and they all clustered darkly together. Even if the leprechaun didn't move the treasure, he seriously doubted that he'd ever find that particular tree again. This, of course, must be what the leprechaun was counting on!

He thought hard. Then he hit on a plan. Tearing a strip of cloth from his shirt, he tied it round the lowest branch of the tree.

"Do I have your word that you won't touch that marker, or take it down?" he demanded.

"By the Blessed St. Patrick and all the holy saints, ye have my word that I won't so much as lay a finger on it!" promised the leprechaun.

This was a powerful oath, and it satisfied the leprechaun's captor. "Very well!" he said, putting the leprechaun down on the ground. "In return for your promise, I'll grant you your freedom." And in the twinkling of an eye, the little man was gone into the bushes nearby and there wasn't a trace of him to be seen. Indeed, he was never seen in that district again.

The man rushed home to get a spade and a pick, in order to dig up the fortune. He was hardly gone more than half an hour and was soon back at the stand of trees, ready for work.

But when he got there, a great shock awaited him. The leprechaun had been busy, all right. Every tree in that particular stand had a strip of cloth tied to its lowest branch, and every strip was exactly the same!

Try as he might, the poor fellow couldn't distinguish one from the other, nor could he remember exactly where the original tree—the one with the fortune at its roots—had been. He dug in several places but always came away empty-handed. Eventually, he had to give up and go back home—his blind sister and aged mother would have to do without the wealth. And as he went, a sound followed him, like the cackling of a bird, hidden away in a bush. Just for a moment, he thought that it might be the leprechaun laughing at him.

More Sinister Uses for Gold

Sometimes, leprechauns would use their immense wealth to entrap mortal souls. Not only would fairy money transform itself into dead leaves, acorns or ashes once the fairy influence had departed; accepting it could damn mortal souls to Hell. Consequently, some leprechauns who steadfastly hated humankind would try to force individuals to accept their coinage, in the hope that they would be so damned. Fairy money was sometimes slipped into ordinary change or given as a reward or payment for some service rendered. Money, therefore, should never be accepted from strangers, and each coin given as change should be thoroughly checked. To ignore this warning could have extremely grave consequences.

The notion of the leprechaun trying to send human souls to Hell closely allies the fairy with the Devil. Rather than being a jolly, drunken, mischievous sprite, the fairy becomes the agent of dark supernatural powers and the enemy of all right-living people.

Although he is primarily portrayed as a cobbler, then, the leprechaun has a number of professions within the fairy world, some of which impinge on the mortal world. He is, in effect, a jack of all trades; and with the weight of such responsibility on his shoulders, he might perhaps be forgiven for his drunkenness and for his surly moods. With such a complicated portfolio, after all, he might be described, in modern-day terms, as being one of the real captains of industry in the fairy world.

PART III

HOW DO LEPRECHAUNS LIVE?

CHAPTER 11

LEPRECHAUN SOCIETY

Although they often give the appearance of being extremely haphazard in their ways, leprechauns are exceptionally well-organized. And although folklorists such as Yeats have classified them as solitary fairies, this organization is predominantly a social one.

Generally speaking, leprechauns are organized into clan groupings that have existed almost since the dawn of time and were certainly established long before the first humans arrived in Ireland. The initial groupings are thought to have followed a rough north-south divide; but as the fairy (and leprechaun) population began to expand, these divisions became much more complicated.

The Four Leprechaun Clans

Although no one is altogether certain, it is thought that there are four major clans within the leprechaun world, roughly corresponding to the four provinces of Ireland—Ulster, Munster, Leinster, and Connaught. To these may be added the clan grouping of County Meath, which was also an ancient province: the lands of the High King at Tara. Within these clan groupings there are a number of subgroupings, but little information on any of these exists. The areas these minor clans inhabit are equivalent to ancient Irish *tuaths* (petty kingdoms or pieces of land held by petty lords for their overall ruler), and are subject to the domination of the larger clans.

Even though very little research has been done on the subject, it is generally assumed that each major clan displays its own unique characteristics, which distinguish it from the others. It is worth examining these characteristics to explore the rich diversity that exists in the leprechaun world.

Ulster Leprechauns

Ulster leprechauns (laughremen) are believed to be the finest storytellers and poets in the fairy world. They have a command of words and imagery that is unequalled anywhere else in Ireland. However, many of their poems and songs are both lengthy and complicated. The great eighteenth-century leprechaun poet Michaeleen O'Coinn, from Slieve Gullion in South Armagh, is said to have composed a work in honor of the harvest that ran to 14,401 verses and took four days and nights to recite in its entirety. Indeed, so complicated was the verse and meter construction of the poem that it could not be memorized or properly recited by any mortal tongue, only by that of a fairy. It is also said that the famous bards of Armagh were initially trained by leprechaun poets, and this gave them their great reputation for the imagery and sweetness of their verse.

Many of the Ulster poems were set to music, and the melodies are so beautiful that they were partly copied by mortals from all over Ireland. Unfortunately, they have long been lost. A similar situation exists in relation to a number of other ancient tunes attributed to the fairy folk: the original texts that accompanied many of these melodies no longer exist, and in most cases, mortal words have been added to the tune.

ULSTER AGGRESSIVENESS

In spite of their reputation for beautiful words and melodies, Ulster leprechauns are among the most aggressive and factious fairies in Ireland. They are incredibly protective of the great wealth they store—which is said to derive from the old kings of Ulster—and they usually suspect that everyone is trying to cheat them out of it. This makes them incredibly defensive and antisocial. They are also reportedly the strongest of all the leprechaun tribes and are terrific sportsmen, excelling at hurling (a favorite leprechaun sport) and soccer. Undoubtedly, their natural aggressive tendencies add to their fierce and uncompromising competitiveness.

Ulster leprechauns are distinctive in their style of dress, often wearing conical or pointed hats as opposed to the soft, wide-brimmed hats worn by other leprechauns. This gives them a malignant and slightly sinister air, which they seem to relish. Some leprechauns in South Armagh do not wear clothing at all; instead, they are covered with a wiry fur, through which their rather wizened faces peer, displaying sharp fang-like teeth. These fairies should not be approached under any circumstances. North Antrim grogochs have already been discussed; they are relatively friendly, but even they can turn nasty if a mortal crosses them. Although they are frequently spotted around riverbanks and under hedges, Ulster leprechauns are probably best avoided.

Connaught Leprechauns

Connaught leprechauns have a reputation for being the most serious and academic of all their kind. While this may be only a rumor, they are said to be highly sober and industrious, spending most of their free time in scholarly study. In fact, it is said that the most notable of Connaught fairies do not drink at all—which is difficult to believe, given the inherent nature of the leprechaun.

> ### LEPRECHAUN ART
> Connaught sprites are said to be deeply interested in art and can be quite artistic themselves when the mood takes them. Examples of their work—usually in the form of indecipherable and wholly abstract paintings—can be found as part of the mosses on some trees or in the strange whorls of the trees themselves.

These leprechauns are the shyest and most mystical of all the fairy folk. They are seen only infrequently and then only by those who cannot harm them ("innocents," very small children, and the seriously drunk). They are very conservative in their ways and shun the colorful dress of their counterparts in other provinces, preferring to clothe themselves in drab hues. They are said to wear plain brown or gray jerkins with cowls, which they often pull over their heads to hide most of their faces, making them look rather like monks. Their specialties are philosophy and literature. They are closely connected with trees, and are often to be seen among the roots of great oaks, absorbed in copying out some book or manuscript.

Their most striking feature is their long beards, which are symbolic of their great age and wisdom—the longer the beard, the wiser and more sagacious the leprechaun. Indeed, some of their beards are so long that they can easily be tucked into the leather belts these fairies wear.

Probably because of their mystical characteristics, Connaught leprechauns are the most secretive of all their kind, choosing to inhabit lonely and inaccessible places—much like the early Christian Fathers. To see one, therefore, is something of a rarity.

Leinster Leprechauns

Leinster leprechauns appear to be the clan upon which the common caricature of the leprechaun is based. They are easily the most drunken of all the species. They dress bizarrely, usually in clashing colors that make them stand out against any background. Consequently, these are the fairies most easily seen by mortals.

They are intensely fond of pranks and spend many of their nights letting out farmers' cattle, overturning their hayricks, or committing other such rogueries about their property. They are inveterate liars, and nothing they say must be believed, nor must any of their oaths be accepted.

Despite their wild and raucous ways, these are the most prosperous leprechauns in all of Ireland. It is estimated that these Leinster fairies have a total of sixteen million pounds hidden away in various locations across the province. Much of this money came from the coffers of the Norman barons who were invited into Ireland by Dermot MacMurrough, King of Leinster, during the twelfth century. Their treasure was hidden away in castles and monastic ruins, and all of these sites are known to the leprechauns of Leinster. Such wealth makes them especially defensive toward humans (and even toward other fairies), and they are regarded as the trickiest of all their kind in Ireland—some folklorists might say they are the trickiest sprites in the whole of the Celtic world.

Leinster leprechauns claim to be the oldest family of their kind in Ireland, and there is no doubt that the original leprechauns came from somewhere within the province. However, this does not excuse their outlandish behavior, and they are generally regarded with a kind of disdain by many other leprechaun clans and by many other fairies across the Irish countryside. Not that this upsets them; indeed, it seems to make them even more rowdy and boisterous in their ways.

LEINSTER REBELS

Leinster leprechauns are widely regarded as the "rebels" of the fairy world, deliberately defying almost every form of generally accepted convention. Perhaps because of their inordinate wealth, they are generally tolerated by other fairies and are widely sought after by greedy mortals.

Meath Leprechauns

Meath leprechauns are well known for their arrogance and snobbery. Although Leinster leprechauns claim to be the oldest of their species in Ireland, this is hotly disputed by members of the Meath fraternity, who claim that they and they alone are the oldest. Furthermore, they claim many connections with the old High Kings of Ireland, who had their seats at Tara, even though there is no real historical evidence for such claims. This, however, does not prevent the Meath leprechauns from putting on airs and graces as though they themselves were royalty.

They have a high opinion of themselves as diplomats, and claim to have interceded in many disputes in ancient Ireland—although this is certainly open to question. They also place a high value on their own eloquence and lay claim to several old ballads and poems that are more properly attributable to their Ulster brethren. They are widely known (and abhorred) for their ability to give long and convoluted speeches at the drop of a hat. They are also extremely curious, to the point of nosiness, and will often involve themselves in affairs that are not properly their concern. They will dispense advice they claim has been "culled from the centuries," but is actually little more than their own overblown opinions.

They frequently set themselves up as arbitrators and mediators in disputes between other fairy folk, relying on their own "great wisdom" to settle arguments. In many instances, such "mediation" fails and the Meath leprechauns resort to age-old strategies—beating both parties into submission with a cudgel, or holding a knife to the throat of one of the parties to force him to make peace with the other. This is what counts as "diplomacy."

Unlike most other leprechauns, the Meath fraternity does not drink poteen with any frequency, preferring either mead or honey beer, which they consider a grand drink and consume with great gusto. The fact that this drink has its origins among the English Saxons does not appear to deter them, and they have been known to quaff copious amounts of English ale with similar relish, claiming it was a drink of the ancient High Kings of Ireland (this is without question false).

> ## MEAD
> Mead, made by fermenting honey with water, is said to be the world's oldest alcoholic drink. There are different varieties; for instance, mead brewed with hops or mixed with beer is called *braggot*. Some mead can be aged to improve its flavor.

The clothing worn by Meath leprechauns is much finer and slightly more color-coordinated than that of their counterparts elsewhere, and this is taken as a sign that they consider themselves to be the "aristocrats" of the leprechaun world. However, like any other leprechauns, their word is not to be trusted. Given the slightest opportunity, they will resort to mischievous tricks and pranks, just like others of their species.

Munster Leprechauns

Munster leprechauns are thieves, ruffians, and robbers. It is often said that they give their Leinster relatives a run for their money when it comes to drinking, but this may be simply boasting on the part of some Munster folklorists. Munster leprechauns are the ones who are most likely to come into contact with humans, since they frequently break into houses to steal whatever they can, eat whatever food has been left untouched, and consume whatever drink happens to be available. It is among these fairies that the highest number of *cluricauns* is to be found.

These leprechauns are famed for their fast thinking and their way with words. They are generally regarded as the sweetest talkers in Ireland, with the ability to charm the fowls out of the air through the power of their words. Conchabhar Thadhg MacRúairí of Clare, the great hedge poet, allegedly learned his skill with words from a Munster leprechaun, as did the wandering poet from County Cavan, Cathal Buí.

(It is said he acquired his fondness for strong drink from the leprechaun too.) Another Clare poet, Brian Merriman, is also said to have been greatly influenced by the Munster sprites. It is well known that Munster fairies have a penchant for exaggerated stories, particularly those regarding themselves. They will portray themselves as great warriors or scholars with such skill that their listeners will totally believe them and will be gripped by the tales of their fictitious exploits.

These fairies are inveterate gamblers and will wager on anything—even on two flies climbing a wall or on the length of a shadow at midday. Many of the fairy fairs and goblin markets throughout Munster have some games of chance; passing mortals can be drawn to these and persuaded to part with their money. Even if a Munster leprechaun should lose at one of these activities, he is so skillful with words that he can usually escape paying out what he has lost and may even manage to persuade his opponent that it is he who has lost the wager.

THE WORST MUSICIANS IN IRELAND

The Munster leprechauns are reputed to be fine musicians and exceptionally sweet singers—although there is no evidence for such a claim. Indeed, many folklorists claim they are the worst musicians and singers in the fairy realm—possibly in all of Ireland (although they are believed to be reasonable dancers)—and put all their artistry into talk and blarney.

It is also said they are among the few of the leprechaun tribe who will actually marry mortal women. However, marriage to a Munster leprechaun is not to be sought, for they, like all leprechauns, are extremely untrustworthy and flighty in their ways. No good can ever come of such unions. It is advisable, given their roguery and wild ways, that Munster leprechauns should be utterly avoided, even though they are the most accessible of the leprechaun species.

Beyond these admittedly sweeping classifications, not very much is known about organization within the Irish leprechaun world. There are known to be a large number of smaller clans and groups, but the leprechauns remain very secretive about how they are structured and their exact functions. It is not even known if they are established along family or kinship lines; but, since many leprechauns appear to bear different names, this seems extremely unlikely. In Scotland, the situation is thought to be slightly different: leprechauns may be organized along lines similar to those of the Highland clans, by connections of family and kin. However, no hard evidence exists for this assumption, which is mainly based upon hearsay and folktale.

Chief and Leaders

In Ireland, there are some hints which lead to certain deductions regarding the structure of leprechaun groupings. For example, each clan, no matter how minor, has a leader, generally known as "Himself," who is the most prominent leprechaun in a given region. Every four to five years, these local leaders are required to swear allegiance to an overlord of the entire Irish leprechaun nation—"the Grand Himself."

Another name for the leader (both national and local) is *Ferganainm*, which literally means "man without a name." In ancient Ireland, this title was used among the Gaelic aristocracy to denote illegitimacy—certain Irish clan leaders, including Ferganainm O'Carroll and Ferganainm O'Neill, used it as a proper name—but folklorists believe that among the fairy kind it may mean something altogether different. In fact, it seems, to be a title of high rank.

We do not know how often the Grand Himself (or Ferganainm) changes, or how his successor is chosen, although it is thought that this might be either by popular vote or by some great feat—such as drinking a barrel of poteen at one sitting.

The loyalty-swearing by the various lower Himselfs is reminiscent of the ancient Ard Feis, during which sub-chieftains swore their allegiance to the Ard Rí (high king) of Ireland in former times. Like this great festival, the loyalty-swearing ceremony takes place over four or five days, during which there is much merriment and a great deal of strong drink is consumed.

The pattern of the festivities is determined by the location where the event takes place. If, for instance, the ceremony is held in Ulster, then it is characterized by a great hurling match and by various feats of strength and physical skill. If it is held in Connaught (and few of them are), it will be characterized by debate, recitation, and the composing of poetry. It has even been noted (although not verified) that some Connaught gatherings are completely "dry"—i.e., devoid of any form of strong drink: the leprechauns there declare that poetry should be "sufficient liquor to intoxicate the soul."

Should the ceremony be held in Munster, its main attraction will be the lies and tall stories of the participants, while those ceremonies held in Leinster (where the majority of them are, in fact, held) are usually no more than drunken brawls. Leinster and Munster gatherings also tend to be marketplaces where "mislaid" property—usually stolen from the homes of mortals—is on sale, games of chance abound, and there is trading, bargaining, and wagering in abundance. In these cases, the swearing of loyalty to the Grand Himself usually takes second place or is even forgotten altogether (as, according to some stories told by old people in Munster, it was in 1897, 1902, and 1931).

PART III: HOW DO LEPRECHAUNS LIVE?

The Ceremonies of Meath

The grandest gatherings are, as might be expected, held by the leprechauns of Meath. Although these are not always strictly leprechaun functions (different kinds of fairies and sometimes the occasional mortal—assuming he or she is of sufficiently high status—are occasionally invited to attend), they epitomize the genteel side of the fairy world. Such occasions, according to other leprechauns, are very "boring," filled with lofty conversations and frequent name-dropping, with none of the drunken merriment that characterizes gatherings in some other provinces. These gatherings are normally shunned by the Ulster, Munster, and Leinster leprechauns, with the Connaught contingent only making a token appearance.

Although all of these meetings (which are supposed to be formal ceremonies) have a haphazard air about them, it is well known that leprechauns are fiercely loyal, both to their clan and to their province. If called upon to perform any task for the local Himself or the Grand Himself, each leprechaun will obey without question. It is inherent in their nature to do so, and this gives a form of structure to their entire society.

In the early days, it is said, there were frequent wars and battles between various clans (and even provinces) of leprechauns, during which local Himselfs called upon their followers to fight for the honor of their regions. Old people will still speak about seeing so-called "fairy fights," either in the sky or in remote places, during which great armies of leprechauns faced each other. The sheer numbers involved speak eloquently of how readily such calls to arms were heeded. Nowadays, although times are much more peaceful in the fairy world, leprechaun leaders still inspire (and demand) almost unquestioning loyalty from those beneath them.

CHAPTER 12

LEPRECHAUN LAW

With any form or organized structure comes the concept of law, and leprechauns are no different in this respect. Like the ancient Brehon laws of Ireland and the Laws of Hywel Dda in Wales, leprechaun laws are not thought to be written down in any coherent or cohesive whole. Nor is there really any unifying principle that defines these laws, since most of them are communally based, pertaining to the specific community in which they are used. It is extremely doubtful whether any of them are actually written down; if they are, it is unlikely that they are transcribed in any codes or books. If they do exist, it is in a scattered and fragmented form not readily accessible to either mortals or the leprechauns themselves. Much of their law, it is suspected, exists only on an *ad hoc* or localized basis.

Most laws are enacted through a tribunal of judges or "casters" (no doubt they take this title from the financial arbiters at human fairs—especially rabbit fairs—and markets across Ireland). The chairman of such tribunals is usually, although not necessarily, a local Himself. The tribunal may comprise the three oldest leprechauns in any given community, but it is more probable that in some areas the members are chosen by drawing lots.

Leprechaun Tribunals

On some occasions, the casters at a court are leprechauns from another locality or province. For example, leprechauns in Ulster may be tried by a tribunal from Munster, and vice versa. Leprechauns from Meath consider themselves great and impartial judges, although this is open to question. They are brought in to sit in a number of fairy courts, but this probably has more to do with their self-perceived high status than with any formal legal expertise. Because of their knowledge of ancient texts and their inherent wisdom and good sense, Connaught leprechauns are much sought after as casters. Even so, the majority of them decline the honor. Few Connaught leprechauns become involved in anything legal; on the whole, they prefer to study things like history and philosophy.

Tribunals are convened only when there is some sort of dispute between leprechauns, or when it is alleged that some sort of crime has been committed. (These are not "crimes" in the human sense; they may include excessive noisiness, long periods of relative sobriety, and so on.) The casters will hear all sides and will deliberate at length (usually over copious amounts of poteen, supplied by the local leprechaun community) before arriving at their decisions. These judgments do not have to be unanimous—a simple majority verdict will do.

From the (admittedly questionable) accounts of those mortals who have secretly witnessed them, leprechaun courts seem to be rather undisciplined affairs, reminiscent of courtrooms in the American Wild West. Strong drink is permitted to be served throughout the proceedings, and this often leads to rowdy and undisciplined behavior among both the spectators and the judges. Indeed, it is said that on a number of occasions, during certain lengthy proceedings, the judges have become so intoxicated that they could not reach a coherent decision. There is also, if reports are to be believed, a great deal of trading and selling between leprechauns within the court, so the whole affair takes on the appearance of a market.

Tribunal Procedure

The casters sit at the head of the courtroom, which is usually an open area in the corner of a field or a ruined building specially designated for this purpose. The chairman of the tribunal carries with him a *bachall*, or staff, suggestive of the ancient Irish Brehons or druids. This is the symbol of his authority, and he will not deliver his judgment without it.

BACHALL ISU

The bachall has Christian connections as well. St. Patrick is said to have brought to Ireland the Bachall Isu, or "staff of Jesus." The staff was allegedly given to Patrick by a hermit living on an island in the Etruscan Sea. It was kept in reverence until the English reconquest of Ireland, when it was burned (presumably as a relic of idolatrous practices) in 1538 on the orders of the Archbishop of Dublin.

There are no lawyers; petitioners are simply called to state their cases, while the tribunal frequently refreshes itself with liquor as it gives due consideration to their pleas. Each petitioner may, if he chooses, bring a number of supporters to urge him on and to add due weight to his case. They are permitted to call out encouragement to those they support and to ridicule the opposition as they see fit. If things get a bit out of hand, Himself is permitted to beat rowdy participants about the ears with his bachall to quiet them down. However, neither Himself nor the casters will be averse to a little bribery, and they are equally vulnerable to intimidation, which may produce a similar result.

Judgments

Judgments issued by leprechaun courts usually involve fines and compensations. Since leprechauns are protective of the wealth that they have stored away, this is a serious deterrent against bad behavior; if the case is a dispute between two sprites, this usually brings about a speedy agreement. In some cases, the head of the tribunal has the right to batter both wrongdoers and disputants about their skulls with his bachall. In cases of disputes or bad behavior, the severity of the judgment is also dependent upon the temperaments and idiosyncrasies of the casters, although certain general principles are usually observed. Crimes of mischief against mortals, for example, are not considered crimes at all, since most leprechauns regard mortals as slow and stupid, while crimes against the fairy population—like a leprechaun being excessively rowdy and making a nuisance of himself—are often regarded with the utmost severity.

Penalties

Since leprechauns are immortal, there is no death penalty under fairy law (for fairies, that is; these courts can pass the death sentence upon mortals—see later in this section). The direst penalties a leprechaun court can issue consist of "being sent to Coventry" (i.e., shut out of all normal fairy relationships and treated with disdain and silence) or, in the most extreme cases, expulsion and exile from the local community. For a leprechaun, banishment to a place where he knows no one is equivalent to a long jail sentence. These sanctions, it has to be said, are not often used, but when they are, it is to great effect. A similar draconian judgment entails depriving the leprechaun of his distilling equipment and forcing him to be "dry" (without liquor of any description) for a specified period.

Leprechaun courts will sometimes pass judgment on humans, particularly if they have committed some slight against the fairies—cutting down a fairy thorn, crossing a fairy path without permission, destroying a fairy rath, or showing disrespect in some other form. Leprechauns consider themselves the protectors of the land (they are, after all, supposed to be manifestations of the ancient land gods of Ireland), and therefore claim jurisdiction over those who despoil it. The penalties their courts impose upon mortals can be extremely severe—utter bankruptcy, twisted limbs or spines, illness, and sometimes even a painful and lingering death. For humans, as for fairies, there is no appeal against the judgment of the court.

Although detailed descriptions of leprechaun courts were mentioned earlier, little is actually known about their system of justice (if, in fact, such a concept exists among them). Indeed, it is generally thought that the formal gatherings described are not called very often, and that when they are, they are not in session for long. No record of leprechaun law has ever been found, and therefore much of our "knowledge" of it consists largely of speculation. Nevertheless, it is still wise to say "By your leave" when crossing a known fairy path, and to leave fairy bushes well alone, lest the full force of the leprechaun legislature fall upon your shoulders.

NO APPEALS

It should be noted that leprechaun law differs from human law in that, once Himself and his casters have made their judgment, there is no appeal against it. To formalize things, the chairman of the tribunal will strike his bachall on the ground, exclaiming loudly, "It is so." The judgment of the leprechaun court is then immutably fixed.

CHAPTER 13

Leprechauns and Religion

When it comes to ghosts and fairies, the Church has sometimes found itself in an invidious and confusing position. It could not very well deny the existence of supernatural creatures, since that might also be to deny that there were evil forces such as demons, but it could not fully acknowledge them either. Furthermore, in many isolated rural areas, old folk beliefs still lingered, and it was better to partially acknowledge the existence of sprites and spirits and bring them under religious control than to have them still secretly worshipped by a local populace in defiance of Church strictures.

Denunciations from the Church

Since a number of ancient texts declared fairies to be the last remnants of the old pagan land gods, the Church in the main was quick to denounce them (and leprechauns in particular) as the servants of the dark powers, closely associated with the Devil himself. However, some religious teachings stated they were fallen angels who would never see Paradise again. This placed them at variance with God and the gradually developing notion of Heaven within the holy mind. No fairy, the Church firmly stated, could enter the heavenly gates. In fact, Church teaching decreed that no supernatural being could enter Heaven unless he or she had some connection to humanity, for whom Christ died. The most common test was to ask if the being had "but one drop of Adam's blood" in his or her veins. The majority of fairies could not claim this and so were excluded from the human afterlife.

"The Priest and the Leprechaun"

Leprechauns were one of the supernatural throng shut out of Heaven, as this old tale from County Down, collected from the great storyteller W.J. Fitzpatrick in 1953, affirms.

Just beyond Moneydarragh Primary School, there was an old priest living at one time. He had been the serving priest in the locality, but he was long retired, although he continued to live around Moneydarragh. His name was Priest O'Hagan, and he was very well liked and very highly respected by the people in the area. He was also extremely wise on all things religious, and the country people still came to him if they had a problem or if they were in trouble. He would always give them a hearing. The house he lived in was a large place, set on its own grounds, which belonged to his family. As Priest O'Hagan grew older, he couldn't manage the place the way he used to, so he employed a serving man called Ned to work about the house and do odd jobs for him.

One evening, Ned was working around the back of the place, where the fields ran down into the priest's garden. There was a big standing stone set into a low bank, just on the very edge of the grounds, which was supposed to be haunted by a fairy. The local people would give it a wide berth, but it never bothered Priest O'Hagan, him being a man of the cloth and all. He was content to let it stand. "It'll be standing here long after I'm in the clay," he used to say.

The sun was going down behind the Mourne Mountains, and Ned was just clearing away the last of the day's work from around the big stone. The shadows were lengthening, and he was uneasy about working there, but he wanted to have everything finished before he went home. Priest O'Hagan was in the house, eating his own supper, and Ned dearly wanted to be by his fireside, doing the same thing.

All of a sudden, he had the feeling that he was being watched, and turning suddenly, he saw someone standing close beside the big standing stone—so close, in fact, that the figure almost seemed to be a part of the stone itself. It was a little man—no bigger than a three-year-old child—with a long skirty coat which reached almost to the ground and a soft, wide-brimmed hat that threw most of his face into shadow. Ned, however, was aware of his eyes, which watched him with a frightful intensity.

There was one other thing about him that made poor Ned's blood freeze. Even in the last rays of the sun, which fell full across the ground, the little man cast no shadow.

Ned knew then that his visitor was one of the leprechauns who were supposed to dwell beside the large stone. He moved to make the sign of the Cross in the air, to ward away evil, but his hand simply would not obey him.

The Leprechaun's Question

"W-what is it that you want from me?" asked Ned, his voice trembling badly.

The little man paused for a moment. "I want you to ask the priest a question," he answered. "For it is said that he is extremely wise on religious matters."

Ned relaxed a little, but he was still wary. He knew that leprechauns could be extremely tricky creatures and were always anxious to entrap mortal souls.

"He is indeed," he answered, a bit more confidently. "There is none wiser on such things in the whole of Ireland. But you can ask him yourself. He is in the house beyond, having his supper."

The little man cast a long glance toward the house. "I would if I could," he replied. "But I fear the collar about his neck and the stink of his holy incense offends me."

In Ned's mind, this confirmed that the being to whom he spoke was indeed a leprechaun.

"Will you ask him a question for me?" the other persisted.

Ned swallowed. "I will, right gladly," he said at last, not wishing to offend the leprechaun for fear of some reprisal. "But Priest O'Hagan is a kind man and will not harm you, no matter who you might be."

"He is still a priest!" retorted the little man. "But since you agree to ask the question, it is this: is there any hope of salvation for me? Ask him if I will ever see the delightful mansions that are said to lie in Paradise. Will you do that for me?"

"I will," replied Ned, still fearful of the other.

"Then I'll come back at the same time tomorrow evening, and you can give me his answer," said the little man.

As he spoke, a bird called in a nearby field, high and shrill, and Ned involuntarily turned to look in its direction. When he turned his head back again, he was alone beside the big standing stone.

He went into the house and found Priest O'Hagan finishing his supper, a holy book propped up on the table in front of him. Ned explained about his meeting with the little man and how the leprechaun had wanted to ask the priest a question.

The Answer

"What did he want to ask me?" asked the old man, with great kindness in his voice.

Ned told him the question, and Priest O'Hagan thought for a long while without ever saying a word. At last he spoke again: "I do not truly know the answer to his question," he said, "but you can tell him this: if he has so much as one drop of Adam's blood in his veins, then he has as much hope of salvation as any man. But if he has not, then salvation is denied to him and he will never see Paradise. That is all I can tell him." And Ned left the old man to his reading.

The next evening, he was finishing his work again, close to the big stone, when he had the feeling he was being watched once more. Turning swiftly, he saw the little man standing among the late-evening shadows close to the stone. Ned's heart nearly stopped within him, but, swallowing, he stepped forward to meet his visitor.

"Well," said the leprechaun, without any sort of greeting, "did you ask him?"

"I did," replied Ned.

"And what did he say?"

"He said that he truly didn't know the answer to your question, but he would tell you this: if you have only a drop of Adam's blood in your veins, you will have as much chance of salvation as any man, but if you don't, then salvation is not for you and you will never see Paradise at all. That was all he could tell you."

For a moment, the little man looked fixedly at Ned, as if taking in his words. Then he crouched down and gave a long, long cry of great sadness. "Ochone! Ochone!" His weeping would have broken your heart to hear it.

At the sound of his cry, a hare started up in the field nearby and went flashing over the grass. Instinctively, Ned turned his head to see it go, and when he turned back, he was alone again. There was nothing there except the big stone, casting its shadow in the late-evening sun.

Ways Around the Ban

As they were to be denied the pleasures of Paradise by virtue of the fact that they had no human blood in their veins, fairies and leprechauns were continually trying to find ways of getting around the prohibition. We have already noted that fairy women who had children by mortal men were always trying to get these babies baptized in the Christian Church, so they might attain the afterlife. Since many of these children are thought to have been leprechauns, it is reasonable to suppose that many leprechauns had hopes of immortality through some sort of Christian immersion. For example, because many baptismal fonts were situated close to the entrances of churches, it was believed that leprechauns sometimes concealed themselves close to the doorways of country churches to catch any of the sacred baptismal water that might be spilled, so they might be baptized in the Christian manner.

"It was said that the leprechauns of Ireland and the other wee folk of the fairy world would never see Heaven," said the great Limerick storyteller Kate Ahern. "But that didn't prevent them from stopping every passing clergyman and asking him if there was any way they could get there. The answer was always the same: if they had even one spot of human blood, they might see Paradise. Not one of them had, and you could hear their cries and lamentations in every old rath and fort all across Ireland. It was a long, low sound, like the wind in the bushes, but it was the cry of the leprechauns that had been denied God's salvation."

THE POWER OF THE HOST

By some it was believed that the crumbs of the sacred Host would attract leprechauns who wished to partake of it in the hope of attaining some form of salvation. (The Host refers to the sacramental wafer used by the Catholic Church during the ceremony of the Eucharist.) Nevertheless, the Church stated that they had no souls and therefore could not receive divine grace, or that they were so wicked and pagan that God had turned His face from them.

Leprechauns and Exorcism

Because leprechauns were often considered to be either servants or actual emanations of the Devil himself, it was essential for the Church to demonstrate its power over them. The way in which it showed its authority over demons and evil presences was through exorcism, and this practice was deemed to apply to leprechauns and the fairy kind as well.

As pagan and Christian myth fused into a generalized folklore, it was widely believed that the very sight of a priest or clergyman could set leprechauns to flight. As is implied in the previous story, leprechauns were greatly frightened even of being in the same room as a man of the cloth. The holiness he exuded was considered anathema to the leprechauns (who were, after all, pagan deities) and would invariably drive them out, even without any form of ritual performed.

A Blessing to Drive Away Leprechauns

However, as folklore developed and became more complex, the mere presence of a holy man was not considered to be enough. Some form of religious rite—a blessing, or the celebration of mass—had to be performed before the leprechauns would leave. There are even tales of leprechauns laughing and mocking the priests and reverend gentlemen who came to expel them from a site. Certainly, in many of the later tales (from around the last century) the leprechauns showed no fear of holy men *per se*. Even the sight of a bishop did not deter them.

Clergymen, therefore, had to recite some form of exorcism to rid any site of fairies and leprechauns. The most popular was the rite for driving away demons and ghosts, since, by the mid-to-late 1800s, these had become connected with leprechauns in the popular mind. The phrases "leprechaun-haunted" and "fairy-haunted" were beginning to creep into the vernacular tongue—the word "haunted" signifying a strong association with ghosts or phantoms.

Exorcisms Against Fairy Malevolence

How could one assess whether or not an exorcism was called for? This judgment was usually based upon both the level and the intent of the leprechaun activities involved. Leprechauns, as we have said, are by nature mischievous creatures, continually playing tricks and pranks upon unsuspecting mortals. It appears that some leprechauns ventured beyond mere mischief and into the realms of actual malevolence. It was against these sprites that the Church extended its power through the holy rite of exorcism.

The "malevolence" the leprechauns showed toward humankind could take many forms. They could, for example, pelt individuals with stones, rocks, and other objects as these humans walked around their property; they could cause burning peats to fall from the fireplace, injuring both humans and animals; they could sing bawdy songs or disclose scandalous things concerning visitors to a house, from secret locations around the rooms (for example, from the chimney); they could break windows and cause hideous apparitions to appear; they could pinch and scratch children as they lay asleep or cause their beds to levitate alarmingly.

> ### POLTERGEISTS
> Poltergeists are mischievous spirits that haunt people's homes. They disrupt household life, flinging objects, moving or losing things, and generally making themselves a nuisance (the name is German for "noisy ghost").

In many ways, leprechaun malevolence paralleled what we would now describe as poltergeist activity. Descriptions of flaming coals flying around the room and of plates leaping from a dresser to be broken on the floor, which seem to be common features of poltergeist phenomena, also match descriptions of leprechaun malevolence toward humans.

The Reverend St. John Seymour, a clergyman who had an interest in the supernatural, mentions an incident in Larne, County Antrim, in 1710, in which leprechauns at a rath near the town invisibly bombarded passersby with stones and foul matter. And the tormenting of the elderly Anne Hattridge (or Haltridge), which began the Islandmagee witch trial in the same county, was initially ascribed to leprechauns alleged to live nearby. In this instance, the movement, in the popular mind, from leprechauns to witches shows how closely the fairies were identified with the powers of evil.

Disrupting Religious Ceremonies

"Malevolence" among leprechauns could also include diverting the pure in heart from thinking about sacred things. For instance, an old story from Limerick describes how, one sunny afternoon, a country priest was dozing in the sunshine with his breviary on his lap, when the leprechauns came and stole the holy book out of his hands. On awakening, the priest, realizing what had been done, cursed them all in God's name, turning them into stones and rocks. This demonstrated the power of the clergy over the pagan sprites. Similarly, many nuns complained of leprechauns pinching them during mass to make them angry and uncomfortable during the Holy Sacrament. Again, this is a clear link to demons and devils.

Formal rituals, involving both pagan and Christian elements, were often performed to drive out leprechauns and other supernatural nuisances.

An Exorcism in Derry

The most complete description we have of such a ritual comes from the town of Derryork in North Derry, and is recounted in the Ordnance Survey Memoirs for the 1830s. A weaver, Joseph MacPhearson, was plagued with leprechauns and other fairy folk from a nearby rath, who interrupted his work with their merriment. He went to plead with them to be quiet, but they only became rowdier, and in time they invaded his house. He could not get near his loom for the number of leprechauns who were partying in his front room.

In desperation, he called the local clergyman, who arrived bearing a Bible and carrying an iron knife. The knife embodies the ancient superstition that all fairies (and leprechauns in particular) fear metal, which was believed to have magical properties. Placing the knife across the open pages of Scripture, the minister (who appears to have been a Protestant) read an Office of Exorcism and dispelled the leprechauns from the dwelling.

The exorcism, however, was largely ineffective: the following night, the leprechauns were back and almost set the house on fire through their carelessness. Many of the locals claimed that it was because a Protestant minister had been brought in—had a Catholic priest delivered the exorcism, it would have had greater effect, they said. Later the leprechauns were to refer derisively to "Joe MacPhearson's leaves and lances" (the pages of Scripture and the iron knife) in their taunting of the poor weaver.

Other Exorcisms

There are also some references to exorcisms carried out by Catholic priests to expel leprechauns from ruined or abandoned churches or other holy precincts where they had taken up residence. In east Tipperary, for example, near the famous (and fairy-haunted) Slievenamon, a rite of exorcism was carried out to drive leprechauns away from a ruined church. However, details of the actual ritual are extremely vague, and there is no indication whether it was successful or not. As time went on, however, leprechauns seem to have become resistant to the banishments of the Church, and rituals against them appear to have been—on the surface, at least—largely ineffective.

It was not only buildings and sites that needed Church exorcism. Sometimes people were possessed. Some leprechauns were said to be so small that they could hide themselves among greenery such as lettuce or cabbage, so that mortals inadvertently ate them in salads or stews. They then took possession of these mortals' bodies, causing them to perform acts they would not normally do.

Added to this, leprechaun malevolence could extend to influencing those who were especially holy, making them do things that were completely out of character. Those who ate with the leprechauns, or who were overly friendly or deferential toward them, were especially at risk.

Sometimes those who refused to do their bidding were equally in jeopardy. Rev. St. John Seymour noted the seventeenth-century case of Lord Ossery's butler (apparently a Sligo man), who refused to play a game of cards with the leprechauns; he had to barricade himself in his house all day "for fear of being possessed by them." When he did eventually set foot outside the door, he was thrown about and dragged out into the fields by some invisible power. He was brought for exorcism to the great Puritan divine, Valentine Greatrakes (the Irish Stroker), under whose eyes he was levitated into the air and suffered great and frequent fits of various sorts under the influence of the leprechauns. A "friendly spirit" later told him to drink the juice of plantain roots to cure himself of one sort of fit, but informed him that he would have to suffer other fits and seizures—and be borne about at the whim of the invisible company of leprechauns—for the rest of his life. The spirit added that if the butler had "acknowledged God in all his ways," he would not have been subject to the fairy power.

In fact, it was widely believed in many rural areas that committing sin invited leprechauns and other fairy creatures to take control of one's life, in much the same way as it was believed that living a godless life encouraged evil to take possession of one's immortal soul. This certainly put the stamp of evil on fairies and leprechauns, as part of the fairy world gradually came to be seen as servants of the Devil and implacable enemies of all godly people.

CHAPTER 14

LEPRECHAUNS AND THE DEAD

The cult of the dead was strong among the ancient Celts and was particularly widespread in Ireland. The *Fáilte na Marbh* (Feast of the Dead—October 31) took on a special resonance in northerly Celtic lands, where the winter days were dark and gloomy and the nights were cold, suggestive of the nearness of the watchful dead. Naturally, this fascination with departed ancestors tinged fairy lore and gave it a sinister edge.

Leprechauns, it was said, had been commanded by God to guard the souls of the dead and convey them to the gates of Heaven, which leprechauns themselves were not allowed to enter. This ritual was known in many country areas as "the fairy funeral." It concerned the spirits of those who had died within the preceding year. At certain times, when the veil between the mortal world and the afterlife was especially thin—such as October 31, Halloween—wandering souls that had been tied to the earth since their demise were rounded up and marched along darkened country roads under a leprechaun escort.

The Fairy Funeral

This was an especially dangerous time for travelers. Should one chance to meet with the fairy funeral, the leprechauns had the power to take the traveler into the afterlife, and the traveler's body would be found by the roadside the following morning. It was generally supposed, too, that the leprechauns would be in a particularly savage and unaccommodating mood at this time, having been forced by divine decree to approach the gates of Heaven without admission while mortals were allowed in. The leprechauns were therefore especially likely to play malicious tricks upon whomever they met. Even to glance out of a window and see this supernatural cavalcade pass was to invite disaster. At worst, the watcher could be left blind or insane; at the very least, a bucket of blood might be dashed in his or her face. It was as well to stay in the house, keeping the doors and windows well fastened and the curtains or shutters closed.

A Nightly Encounter

Nevertheless, there were those who, for one reason or another, braved the roads on nights when the fairy funeral was said to be abroad, and many stories about encounters with the eerie procession have passed into Irish country folklore. Margaret Gallagher, from outside the village of Belcoo in County Fermanagh, relates the following story concerning her grandfather, Pat Gallagher:

"My grandfather was coming home one night from a céilí in Drumcully, beyond Belcoo, on the way to Garrison. He was coming round the roads when he met with the fairy funeral. He knew what it was, for he could hear the crying and wailing of those souls from the area that the fairies were taking with them. He saw a number of little men in long, long coats walking in front of the procession like undertakers at an ordinary funeral. He was greatly frightened and pulled himself up on the ditch so they would pass him by.

He knew what to say, or he would have been taken with them into the Beyond. He turned his coat inside out and said, 'My back from you, my face to you,' and they passed him by without seeing him at all. He always said he had a very lucky escape, all right, for he could have been taken away with them."

Not all travelers on the nighttime roads were as lucky as Pat Gallagher. There are plenty of stories of those who met with the fairy funerals and were carried off by the leprechauns, or were forced to perform some gruesome task before being returned to the mortal world. For instance, the traveler might have been forced to carry a coffin—or, worse, an unshrouded corpse—upon his back for the length of the night, or to some burial spot designated by the leprechauns.

Teig O'Kane

The story of the unfortunate Teig O'Kane from County Leitrim is well known. Throughout the length of a Halloween night, "little men" forced poor Teig to stumble along gloomy, unlit roads and country lanes, carrying a dead body on his shoulders, desperately trying to find a burial place for it. In the most common version of the story, the leprechauns he meets are described as being small, "about the height of a child," and dressed entirely in gray. They have "a wicked way about them," and are exceptionally violent toward Teig, kicking him and beating him with sticks. They are certainly no jolly cobblers, and this probably reflects the leprechauns' surly and envious attitude at this particular time of the year.

Freeing the Dead

Some stories also mention it was possible for certain mortals to remove the spirits of the recently dead from the ghostly throng and bring them home again. To do this, the mortal had to outwit the leprechauns by using some sort of charm or spell (such as the incantation used by Pat Gallagher) that would render him or her invisible. (Hen dung was considered a particularly effective "charm" against the leprechauns who guarded the dead.) There are several tales of husbands whose wives had died (or appeared to have died), yet these men were able to snatch their wives back as the leprechauns passed by the couples' doors. This reversal of death may have been connected with catalepsy, which often gave the victim a deathlike appearance, or with the temporary effects of some disease.

After any encounter with a leprechaun—or any member of the fairy race—in a fairy funeral or not, it was advisable to attend mass as soon as possible, or at the very least consult and receive blessing from a priest. This was in case evil magic should somehow taint the individual and so damn his or her immortal soul. Alternatively, one could run home, kneel, and recite the Lord's Prayer, which would "stay" the evil until mass could be observed. Sometimes a ritual exorcism had to be performed in the house where the person who had met the leprechauns lived, in case he or she had somehow "contaminated" the place with fairy magic.

The notion of leprechauns harked back to the old pagan gods of the earth, and leprechauns were not fairies with whom the Church was especially comfortable. Despite their often jocular and mischievous ways and appearance, they were considered to be emanations of evil forces, and to be avoided. It was advisable to keep a crucifix or a holy medal about one's person or home in case one should encounter a leprechaun. When met with such religious artifacts or with holy prayers, it was said, the sprite would "vanish away like the smoke from a chimney." That was what the Church taught, at least.

"Power over the Dead"

The following story reflects the power the leprechauns sometimes had over the souls of the dead. Elements of the descriptions of the fairies reflect the dwarfish German metalworkers. The story itself comes from Galway.

Near the old church at Kilmacduagh, there is a long bridge over a river. Just beyond the end of this bridge a forge once stood. It belonged to two brothers named Gregory, who were locally famous blacksmiths. However, they were both great drunkards, and in the end they had to give up smithing completely on account of bad health.

The old forge went to wrack and ruin, and never a one went near it, for it was said far and near that the place was badly haunted. When houses, churches, or blacksmiths' forges are left to their ruin, they draw ghosts and phantoms to them—that's a well-known fact. They said that on certain nights of the year—the old festival seasons—there were lights about it, coming and going, like men carrying lamps and lanterns. It was said, too, that you could hear men talking and arguing even though there was nobody there. There were those who would have told you that the place was fairy-haunted, and that little men in bottle-green coats and old-fashioned three-cornered hats and knee-britches could be seen there at all hours of the day.

But it was at night that it was at its most ghostly. There's many that said they could hear the sound of a hammer striking on iron as soon as the sun started to go down, as though men were making horseshoes there. Nobody would go near it, even between the lights (at twilight), for fear of what they might see, for there were queer, broken shadows all about the old place.

There was a man called Anthony Hynds who lived over beyond the bridge, and when he had drink on him, he was afraid of nothing and would do anything for a dare. One evening in the pub, when he had a right drop about him, some of his neighbors wagered him that he wouldn't go up to the old forge and take a look in.

Halloween

Now it was near to Halloween, which is always a bad time of the year for ghosts and fairies. It is said that around this time, the leprechauns have the power to take you away with them into the Beyond, and it is well to stay close to your fire and not go venturing about places that are known to be haunted. But Anthony Hynds had the drink-courage on him and would chance anything, so he readily agreed to the wager.

That night, when it was dark and the moon was covered with clouds, he made his way up to the old forge, with his neighbors following a good way behind him to make sure he carried out the wager. It was a lonely place, sure enough, with the wind sighing in the branches of the old trees that grew around it, like the cry of a banshee. And there were lights coming and going about the smithy, as though somebody was moving about there by the glow of lanterns.

The drink-courage left Anthony Hynds and the sweat stood on his brow like drops of rain, but he'd made a wager with his neighbors and he had to go through with it. He walked along a little lane that led down to the forge and stopped in the shade of a great tree to see what was going on. He could barely believe his eyes.

GRAY AND RED

There's always something odd about a gray horse or a red-headed woman, for it's said that the leprechauns and the fairy kind always have power over those who meddle with either of them.

There around the forge were gathered a number of little men—ugly-looking, they were, with long, long coats on them and old soft hats such as people wore long ago. The forge was lit, and Anthony could see their faces in its red light—cruel-looking, they all were, to a man. He knew then that they were either fairies or leprechauns and that they were shoeing their horses for a night's mischief.

But there was more: there were two men working at the forge, hammering the metal by the light of the forge flames and the glow of a rushlight. Anthony Hynds said ever after that he knew both the men who worked there, and he said both of them had died within the year that had just gone. One, he was certain, was Richard Gregory, who used to own the forge and who had died in drink; the other was a man named Lehane, who had died when he was thrown from a gray horse beside the old church at Kilmacduagh.

Those that die in drink leave their souls open to the abuses of the fairy people. That was the way of it, as Anthony Hynds well knew. He saw that if the two men—or ghosts, as they were—did not work fast enough, one of the rough little men would hit them with a switch he'd cut from a hedge to make them work faster.

Anthony let a great yell out of him at this terrible sight, turned on his heels, and ran back along the lane, the drink-courage completely deserting him. He never stopped until he had reached the road and was safe among the neighbors who had followed him. Only then did he look back, and when he did, he saw the whole place was totally in darkness.

Yet many a one would tell you that when they passed by the old forge, even long afterward, they could see strange lights coming and going and they could hear the sound of hammers striking on metal, as the leprechauns made the souls of them that were recently dead shoe their fairy horses. That was always the way of it, and it's one of the things the Church won't tell you about.

This story portrays the leprechauns as smiths and reveals them to be extremely bad-tempered and cruel, much like the German *kobolds*. While they are certainly not miners in the kobold tradition, the leprechauns display some of the characteristics of these evil dwarves— they employ ghosts to do their work for them, and they treat them abominably. In many tales, these fallen spirits are condemned to serve the leprechauns until the Day of Judgment, as a punishment for their wayward lifestyles when alive.

CHAPTER 15

OTHER WEE CREATURES

Leprechauns are not the only tiny creatures to inhabit Ireland and Great Britain. There are tales from time far distant of creatures who live in hedges, mounds, and elsewhere.

Grogochs, Pechts, and Other Creatures

"The pechts and grogochs came from Scotland, surely," stated Robert McCormick, an old man from the town of Ballycastle on the northern coast. "They came here by way of a land-bridge which was between Kintyre and Antrim in the old days. When the Celtic people came to Scotland, they drove the pechts in front of them and they had to get out of the country. So they came to Ireland, where nobody was living at the time, and started to make their homes here. The Celtic people followed them across the bridge and started to put down roots too. So the pechts had to hide away in secret places around the countryside, and that's why you never see much of them. That bridge of land is long gone, but the pechts are still here. We call them 'fairies' and 'wee people,' and that's how they came to North Antrim and to Ireland as well."

Setting aside some of the more fanciful details, there may be some truth in this notion. Both Scottish and Hebridean folklore are filled with tales of communities of little folk living in remote places, some of whom may have migrated to Ireland in prehistoric times. Some of these may well have been aboriginal peoples displaced by incoming Celtic settlers. Indeed, the general descriptions of the grogochs or pechts seem to confirm this notion.

Grogochs

Although they are widely regarded as a type of leprechaun, the grogochs differ from the standard leprechaun in appearance and character. They are small and brutish-looking, with flat faces and large, languid eyes. They do not wear clothes; instead they grow long, reddish, matted fur covering their entire bodies. They are untidy and dirty in their habits—their fur, for example, is tangled with twigs and straw that the grogochs inadvertently pick up on their travels.

"When I was a wee child and staying with my granny in the Glens [of Antrim]," recalled the famous Waterfoot historian and storyteller Mary Stone, "we would come in from the fields and my granny would say, 'Ye look like an oul' grogoch.' I never knew what that meant, but she always started to comb and untangle my hair. Later on, I found out it meant 'untidy,' because the grogoch is always very untidy and dirty in his habits. He always has bits and pieces of straw and chaff in his hair, and I suppose that after a day playing in the hay fields, I was dirty and untidy too."

Their dwellings were usually piles of tumbled rocks, sometimes no more than two great standing stones pushed over to provide a rude shelter from the elements. Several of these "grogoch's houses" still exist on Rathlin Island, off the Northern Irish coast.

"The Groigock's House is two big stones near Leg-an-thass-nee," reported Rathlin man Frank Craig. "They said you would have been fit one time to see ('one could see') the groigocks lying out on the grass and sunning themselves there. It's up near the Knockans. There used to be plenty of them up there. Leg-a-goin, too: they'd be out sunning themselves, clear as day. When it rained, they took shelter in the House. Two stones leaning together. It's there yet."

Helpful Spirits

Unlike the majority of the leprechaun species, the grogoch does not possess an overly surly nature. This makes him different even from those fairies whom he most closely resembles—the laughremen of the South Armagh region (small, hairy creatures who possess eminently unsociable dispositions and sometimes play tricks on, or show violence toward, humankind) and an unspecified fur-covered entity who dwells in remote areas of County Sligo (who continually torments both animals and small children). In fact, the grogoch is usually helpful to the point of being a nuisance, and will sometimes attach himself to one particular individual or household that he has developed a special affection for. In former times, grogochs would help both Rathlin and North Antrim farmers with the harvest.

The Grogochs As Hard Workers

The grogochs were tireless workers; however, they could not tolerate laziness or idleness in others and frequently took steps to rouse a dozing farmhand or careless worker. Frank Craig relates a story from Rathlin that demonstrates this particular fairy trait:

There was a groigock in John Vawnilds' place over at the Castle Quarter (also known as Bruce's Castle). He was a wee hairy man who would do turns about the place for John and his wife; he would wash spuds for them and take home the cows of an evening.

Now, at this time, John was an old man and liked his rest well enough, especially on a Sunday morning when he should have been at mass. He would take a bit of a lie-in after a week's hard work. But the groigock wouldn't have that at all. When old John was lying snoring in the bed, he would hoist himself up onto the covers and creep up. Then he would batter the old man about the face until he got up and did a bit of work before going to mass. They can't stand anyone not working, do you see?

It was the same when the boys in the fields would sit down to have a rest or a can of tea as they did in the olden days. The groigocks would creep up behind them and torment them until they had to go back to the threshing or whatever they were doing. It got so that the groigocks were great pests and the farmers wouldn't want them about, no matter how good workers they were. And poor John Vawnilds had reason to curse them as well.

That's a true story, for I mind (remember) my grandfather telling that story often. Of course, you don't see groigocks about any more, so I suppose them that sleep late in their beds or in the hay fields are safe enough.

CHAPTER 15: OTHER WEE CREATURES

Always eager to please, grogochs would sometimes make a mess of the tasks they were given, if only through their enthusiasm. A story that was widely told in the Ballycastle area made this point:

A shepherd who worked on Knocklayd Mountain had come into Ballycastle on business. It was the first time in over a year that he had been away from his herd, and as he was going to be all day in the town, he had to find somebody to look after his flock. The sides of the mountain are very steep, and young lambs would be wandering all over the place and falling into ravines or sinking into bogs. Somebody had to be there to see that they came to no harm and to round them up if need be.

WELL-MEANING BUT STUPID
Unlike the standard leprechaun, the grogoch was widely thought to be extremely stupid—a kind of North Ulster "village idiot."

On the top of Knocklayd, there was an old grogoch living, and he was very friendly and helpful, so the shepherd went up and asked him if he would look after the sheep and lambs. The grogoch came to the mouth of his cave and told him he'd be delighted to do so. The shepherd took him down the mountainside and showed him the sheep, grazing on the slopes, and the pen into which they would have to be put at night. The grogoch told him not to worry, that everything was safe in his hands.

The next morning, the shepherd took himself off to Ballycastle, leaving the grogoch in charge. Before he left, he told the fairy to gather all the sheep and lambs in that night, and not to let any wander down onto the lower slopes. Again, the grogoch told him not to worry—he had been herding sheep off and on for hundreds of years—and so the shepherd eventually set off for the town.

He was far longer in Ballycastle than he'd planned to be. The business took up most of the day, and then he ran into some old friends who took him to the pub and bought him drink. The banter among them was good, and so it was late when the shepherd set out and nearly morning when he arrived back on Knocklayd Mountain.

To his surprise, all the sheep and their lambs were in the pen, with the grogoch looking after them. However, the little man seemed greatly out of breath and looked very tired. The shepherd naturally asked him if he'd had any trouble with the flock.

The Brown Lamb

"No real trouble," the grogoch answered him. "I got them all gathered in without too much trouble, although a wee brown lamb wouldn't go into the pen and I had to chase it all over the mountain nearly all night. I caught it at last and put it in the pen with the others, but it took me some time to get it in, all right. It didn't want to go."

This puzzled the shepherd, for he knew that there was no brown lamb among his flock, and he told the grogoch so. The other, however, insisted that the brown lamb was there and brought the shepherd over to the pen to see it. Imagine his astonishment when he saw, lying in the shadow of the circling stone wall, nothing more than a small, out-of-breath hare. The stupid grogoch, unable to tell the difference between a lamb and a hare, had chased it all over Knocklayd for the whole night!

In spite of their stupidity, the grogochs were extremely good-hearted and eager to do good turns. Indeed, they were so eager to please that they invariably became pests about the house. They would run about (often invisibly) trying to do small chores for the woman of the house, and would usually end up creating more mess than they cleared. When a housewife unaccountably stumbled or tripped in the kitchen, she was sure she had stepped on or bumped against an invisible grogoch. The great Rathlin Island storyteller Rose McCurdy mentioned such an encounter:

Did nobody tell you about the gruogock? That's what they call them on this island and on parts of the mainland as well. I had a man from the County Sligo come to see me, and he knew what it was. In Ireland, where I come from [the inhabitants of Rathlin Island always refer to the mainland as "Ireland"; Rose was born in Glenshesk, outside Ballycastle], they called him the grigock, but it's this land [Rathlin] that I'm talking about now.

There was a grigock's house up at Clegganleck on the upper end of the island. He was supposed to come down from it every day at one time—Alex Morrison or Owney Murphy will tell you the truth of it, for they seen him many a time. The woman of the house was polluted with the grigock coming down to her every day. When she got up from her chair, he would rise up with her and would be round her legs and feet. And he was always running 'round the fire and getting in her way. She was polluted.

One day, she was carrying a kettle of boiling water from the fire and the grigock was running around her feet, and what did she do but spill a drop on him. He let out a screech of a yell, they said, and shouted in the old Irish (which was all that he spoke), "Oh! Oh! My viggerald-vaggerald is all scalded!" That's what it sounded like. And he ran out of the house and all the way back to Clegganleck. But I would bet that the grigock never came back to that house again, nor did he go near any of the houses after that.

No Rewards

Unlike other leprechauns, the grogoch was not interested in either money or reward for his labors. In fact, any sort of money or gift was anathema to him, and to offer him such a reward, even out of gratitude or sympathy, would invariably drive him away from a house. Frank Craig elaborated on this in a famous tale of the grogoch, widely repeated on Rathlin Island.

There was a grogoch worked over at Douglas Cecil's place at times during the year. One time, there was a very harsh winter, with snow lying all over the island, but the grogoch came down from his house and worked away. Old Mrs. Cecil—her that's long dead—that was the woman of the house, took pity on him and said it was a shame to have the grogoch doing everything for them and not getting a haet ("whit") back for his troubles, and him such a good worker and all, and the weather being so cold. So she was spinning this day and had a wee bit of the wool left over from what she was making. She thought that she'd make something for the grogoch. There was enough wool to make a pair of heavy socks for him, and she left them out the next time he came by.

When he got them he began to cry.

"Do you not like them?" asked old Mrs. Cecil.

And the answer he gave her was that he could never get back again. "When yous give me a reward," says he, "I can never come back again. I can't get back."

And he went away crying. That was the last the Cecils or anyone else saw of him ever again.

Ancestors of the Leprechauns?

The nature and stories of the grogoch have been explored here in some depth, as the creature may give some hint as to the origins of the leprechaun. The primitive conditions in which the grogoch lives—under standing stones, in caves, or in deep ravines—are suggestive of a reclusive aboriginal race that may have migrated to Ireland from Scotland or elsewhere, and who coexisted with the Celtic peoples for a long time. Their overall appearance adds to this theory. There are a number of stories of grogochs working for and trading with country people, and this may be some sort of memory of the interchange between the two races in some former time. Moreover, the grogoch belongs to a tradition of small people and diminutive communities that is widespread all over Scotland and the Hebrides.

Hebridean Brownie

Not all such races are deemed to be as slow-witted or as good-hearted as the grogoch—indeed, some are considered to be very wise and crafty in their ways. On the Hebridean island of Colonsay, legends of a particular brownie abound. Although no description of him exists, he is believed to be a small old man who lives in a secluded part of the island or on one of the neighboring tidal islands, Oronsay or Cara. It was thought that island witches sometimes consulted this fairy to find out future events or locate lost property within the community. Other tales make him the moral overseer of island life: those who have wronged their neighbors are sure to be punished by the brownie; those who are neglectful of their work may receive a sharp reprimand (in the form, perhaps, of a small accident or mishap) to remind them of their duties. To keep on the right side of the sprite, local people would leave an offering for him—a libation of milk or whiskey—at a large rock near the center of Colonsay. The method of making this offering was quite specific. The person offering the libation came to the place at night, poured it into a hollow in the middle of the rock and then walked away. On no account should he or she look back, for fear of seeing the brownie and inviting bad luck upon himself or herself—for the little man had miraculous powers and could call down a curse on the viewer. Invariably, the offering disappeared.

Rúairí MacNeill of Barra

Similar beings, all with peculiar magical skills, existed on many other islands in the Hebrides. The celebrated Hebridean pirate, Rúairí MacNeill of Barra, is believed to have consulted a little fairy man on the island of North Uist before several of his raids.

At the end of the sixteenth century, MacNeill had received letters of marque and reprisal from the English court to enable him to attack French and Dutch shipping. After consulting with the fairy creature, however, he changed his tactics: he began to attack Irish shipping and ravaged townships all along the coast of Cork. This brought him to the attention of Queen Elizabeth I, who complained of the pirate's activities to King James VI of Scotland. The Scottish king designated Roderick MacKenzie, who afterward became the Tutor of Kintail, to hunt MacNeill down. The little man in North Uist, however, assured the pirate that he would never be captured, and MacNeill had the misfortune to believe the word of a fairy. He was captured by MacKenzie at Kismul Castle on Barra; and though his life was spared and he was allowed to keep his lands, he had to acknowledge MacKenzie as his overlord and give up piracy, which had been a profitable source of income for him. Legend says that the island of North Uist rang with the spiteful laughter of the fairy man: he had humbled the MacNeill noble, which had been his intention all along.

Other Leprechaun Cousins

Throughout the Outer Hebrides, such creatures are known either as *talla* (a Highland Gaelic word for "echoes," since they are supposed to be reflections or echoes of humankind) or *iridich nan creag* ("the gnomes of the rock"). They live in small communities or as solitary fairies, keeping well away from human places, for which they have a particular aversion. They are regarded as being extremely spiteful, seeking only to cause mischief against humans. In appearance, they often resemble the traditional stereotype of the Irish leprechaun, and it may well be that the image of the Irish fairy is derived from his Scottish counterpart. Certainly, he belongs to a general corpus of folklore that stretches between the two countries.

THE FAIRY OF MAN

The leprechaun has also connections on the Isle of Man, where a fairy known as the Little Old Man of the Barn exists. This sprite is extremely reclusive, but like the grogoch in North Antrim, is extremely helpful to farmers around the Peel area of the island. He works only at night, threshing corn in farmers' barns in return for a libation of milk or whiskey or for a small portion of food. He is also to be greatly feared, for when crossed or angered, he can cause drought or sickness in livestock. Generally, however, he is a beneficent spirit and will only react maliciously if someone refuses to leave an offering or acts irresponsibly within the community.

PART III: HOW DO LEPRECHAUNS LIVE?

Viking Ancestors

The leprechaun may have another point of origin, this one within the Viking world.

The Norsemen had a highly developed mythology which included giants, monsters, wizards, fighting men and diminutive races. Their dwarfish races—simply known as dwarves—were extremely wise and skilled and worked mainly as ironsmiths. They constructed magical helmets, armor, and chains, which adorned many of the Scandinavian heroes. They dwelt far under the earth in volcanic pits (which were their forges) and kept well away from surface-dwellers. However, they could be consulted by and offer advice to other races when the need arose. For example, when the wolf-demon Fenris tormented Asgard (the seat of the Norse gods), the deities asked the dwarves to forge

CHAPTER 15: OTHER WEE CREATURES

an unbreakable chain that would bind the creature for eternity. This the dwarfish smiths did, using exotic substances such as the spittle of birds and the beard of a woman, and using the magical chain, the gods were eventually able to bind Fenris.

Dwarves also appear in some of the other Viking sagas, and they are regarded as extremely wise, if somewhat devious, creatures. They were also believed to be the final custodians of arcane knowledge and practices.

Such beings eventually became incorporated into the folklore of other races. For example, the Viking dwarves probably metamorphosed into the *trows* of Orkney and Shetland—small, usually solitary, highly malignant creatures who inhabited remote islands and sites scattered all through the northern waters. Trows are believed to be extremely ugly and dirty; they may help humans if they have a mind to, but they are more likely to create some mischief. They are also often regarded as extremely drunken in their ways, and this may reflect their Viking origins—Viking dwarves were always paid with a jug of mead or spirit.

So how did Viking folklore come to influence the folk beliefs of Ireland?

Between the ninth and eleventh centuries, Ireland was probably one of the most important Norse bases in the Sudreyjar (the Southern Isles). A number of large Viking colonies existed, mainly in the south of the country; these were the forerunners of such modern cities as Dublin, Limerick, Waterford, Wexford and Cork. From these colonies, raiding ships sailed out to wreak havoc against shipping and settlements along the English and Welsh coasts, and Viking bands extended their influence and culture into the surrounding countryside. They captured portions of Irish land to extend their city-states; they made alliances with local Irish chieftains; and they married Irish women. In time, a new line emerged among the Irish people—the Gael-Goidl (the foreign Gaels), who were a cultural hybrid of Norse and Irish influences.

Norse Legends

Undoubtedly some of the Norse belief systems passed into the common Irish cultural stream through this new stratum of society, and with them, legends of dwarves and diminutive men may also have been incorporated into the Irish folk tapestry. Such tales may have mingled with dimly remembered stories of aboriginal dwarf communities the Celts had encountered, either on their arrival in Ireland or on their journey there. The two stereotypes may well have fused to create a small, low-set man, a custodian of ancient lore and traditions, skilled in the ways of some craft, who was always tricky and cunning as far as mortals were concerned. Recalling the clinkers of the dwarf ironsmiths' fires, this character was always dirty and disheveled. He was also invariably disreputable, preferring his own company to that of other sprites. He was, in fact, the archetypal leprechaun.

CHAPTER 16

THE CLURICAUN AND OTHERS

It would be extremely remiss to conduct any discussion of the leprechaun without mentioning the *cluricaun*. Although many leprechauns deny all knowledge of such a being or treat him with indifference or disdain, he is in fact closely related to them. In fact, some folklorists have described him as "the leprechaun's first cousin."

A fleeting reference to the cluricaun has already been made in connection with Munster leprechauns. Most cluricauns are to be found in Munster, although there are reports of them in other provinces as well. The cluricaun shares several of the leprechaun's characteristics; many who have seen both of them claim it is difficult to tell them apart.

Differences Between Leprechauns and Cluricauns

The main differences between leprechauns and cluricauns are those of fashion and temperament. While the leprechaun pays little attention to dress and style, preferring mismatched clothing reminiscent of artisan garb, the cluricaun dresses in more flamboyant garments. While the leprechaun has a preference for subdued, natural shades (which will camouflage him much better out of doors), the cluricaun puts on more striking and gaudy colors, having a special affinity for red and plum hues. While the leprechaun closely resembles the artisan which he is supposed to be, the cluricaun has the air of a down-at-heel gentleman out on a spree. Although colorful, his clothing is rather shabby and dusty, patched with pieces of material of different shades. His shoes, though buckled, are often scuffed and worn, with the soles coming away from the uppers (something which deeply shocks even the most easygoing leprechaun).

Appearance

The cluricaun's skin is much ruddier than that of the leprechaun (leprechauns are frequently believed to be slightly pallid), giving him a perpetually drunken appearance. Sometimes, although not always, he is inclined to be hairier; and in contrast to leprechauns, who are mostly clean-shaven, he allows his beard to grow to a great length—on occasion, he can tuck it into his belt, in the fashion of Connaught leprechauns. Rather than smoking a dudeen, he is given to puffing upon a foul-smelling "Danish pipe" (an old-fashioned, sometimes ornamented, long-stemmed pipe), which he fills with some indefinable mixture.

CHAPTER 16: THE CLURICAUN AND OTHERS

While the leprechaun is industrious and surly, the cluricaun is idle but extremely cheery. Inordinately fond of strong drink, he resembles the sot who frequently props up the corner of the bar in public houses. Like many drunks, he regards himself as a bit of a dandy and irresistible to women, be they mortal or fairy.

The cluricaun is also a robber, stealing from mortal homes. While the household is asleep, he will break in and take what he can—usually drink or food. Through his magic, he will enter wine cellars or pantries, even locked cupboards, and help himself to whatever bottles of liquor he can find. This explains why the level of drink in some bottles seems to fall inexplicably over the course of a few nights. He will also gorge himself upon leftover pie or fowl, or whatever bread or potatoes he can find. Usually he will not take money, but he is attracted to shiny things and gaudy jewelry, which he will sometimes take away with him. When he has tired of these, he will sometimes (although not always) return them, hiding them in rather inaccessible places around the house—down the back of an armchair, or in some infrequently opened drawer. He is not malicious; he is more of a nuisance than anything else.

> **THE DUDEEN**
> In addition to being a short clay pipe, smoked by leprechauns and others, the dudeen also lends its name to a traditional Irish reel, "The Old Dudeen," first recorded in 1949.

Cluricauns do not carry money, nor do they have any knowledge of hidden hoards of gold. They simply steal or take what they want with impunity. This sometimes makes them vulnerable to capture by vigilant mortals. If caught, however, the cluricaun can usually charm himself out of any situation, mainly by force of his cheery personality and his way with words. Should his captor's gaze be diverted, even for the briefest moment, then the cluricaun—like his leprechaun cousin—will vanish almost immediately. Consequently, if he is cornered, most of his admittedly pleasant conversation will be designed to divert and distract his captor so he can escape.

Storytellers and Drinkers

There is no doubt that cluricauns are grand company. They are regarded as great storytellers and have a collection of tales stretching back into the mists of antiquity, which will astound and delight the listener. If cornered, the cluricaun will invariably suggest his captor "open a bottle" with him so they can resolve the matter "over a glass, like two civilized beings." Here the mortal needs to be wary, for the cluricaun's capacity for strong drink far outstrips that of a human being; he will still be regaling the company with his stories long after every mortal present has passed out. He will then go on to empty all nearby casks and bottles, as well as the pantry (cluricauns have prodigious appetites), before taking his leave.

Angry Cluricauns

Because of their rather drunken and easygoing temperaments, cluricauns are extremely slow to anger; but when they are roused, their wrath can be quite fearsome. They can turn the milk completely sour overnight, prevent hens from laying, or inflict terrible wasting diseases upon a household. They can make cattle fall ill, and sheep break out of their pens. They can cause minor disasters about a house—from the simple breaking of windows to the collapse of a chimneystack. Although they will not willingly cause death, some of the sicknesses which they inflict can be very severe—poxes of various types, fevers, chills—and they can even cause dangerous accidents about the farmyard. It is, therefore, not wise to cross a cluricaun.

Alternatively, the cluricaun can bring good fortune to a house, if the mood takes him—this is not common, but it has been known to happen. Anticipating this, many householders will leave out a little piece of bread or a little saucer of milk or poteen for the fairy. This offering is meant to curry favor with the sprite and to keep him from raiding pantries or cellars. If the cluricaun is pleased with the gift, he may leave a coin (undoubtedly stolen from somewhere else) as payment, or he may simply lay a spell of good fortune on all the members of the household. In many cases, he will also act as the protector of the dwelling, seeing off evil spirits, ghosts and bad luck.

A Cluricaun's Temperament

The cluricaun can often be much more capricious, temperamental and unpredictable than his leprechaun counterpart. In his drunken state, his mischief can sometimes get out of hand; for his own amusement, he will create mayhem throughout the house during the hours of darkness—overturning chairs, opening cupboards and wardrobes, pulling down plates and frightening the animals in their byres. It is doubtful whether he means any harm by this behavior—it is usually put down to mere drunkenness—but he certainly can create a mess and much confusion. Not only this: the cluricaun, "for sport," will also harness sheep, goats, cattle, sheepdogs and even domestic fowl, and ride them all through the countryside in a single night until the animals are dropping with fatigue and are fit for nothing. He will also break down fences and walls, and he often chases cattle through the countryside, making additional work for the farmer. Then, from the shadow of a sheltering hedge, with a jug of stolen poteen at his side, he will laugh at the mortals as they try to repair the damage he has caused. Again, the saying in the country is that "there is no harm in him," that he simply takes his mischief to excess, but there is no doubt that the cluricaun can cause great upset in any community.

Leprechauns and Cluricauns

Leprechauns have no great love or respect for their distant cousin, nor do they condone his "pranks," for which they are frequently blamed. As has already been noted, leprechauns are not above such mischief themselves, but they usually only get up to it at certain times of the year (when they are at their most drunken), and they strongly object to being blamed for activities for which they are not actually responsible. Consequently, they tend to treat the cluricaun as a rogue and a scoundrel and refuse to acknowledge any form of kinship with him. They denounce his activities and treat him with a lofty disdain—particularly the more serious and academically inclined Connaught leprechauns, who tend to regard his inebriated escapades with the utmost horror. Some even deny that he exists at all.

Not that the cluricaun cares a fig about what they may think of him. He is out to enjoy himself if he can. Indeed, he may even go so far as to encourage the notion that has developed among some fairy watchers—that cluricauns are nothing more than leprechauns out for "drunken divilment."

Sheela-Na-Gigs

Although sheela-na-gigs are not really considered part of the fairy pantheon, there is a certain strand of Irish folklore which suggests that, in their initial form, they may be distantly related to the leprechaun. Academics, of course, will strenuously dispute this, claiming that they are representations of some ancient fertility goddess connected with reproduction and rebirth, but one is never sure. So it is probably wise to include some reference to them here.

ANCIENT FEMALE LEPRECHAUNS?
Even though it has been asserted that there are now no female leprechauns, this may not always have been the case. Perhaps in some aboriginal time, when the fairy world was beginning to emerge out of its prehistoric past, there were female variants of a historically remote leprechaun ancestor. Some of these variants may even have survived until the early medieval period, and may have had an influence upon early Christian religious art. Since then, however, they appear to have become extinct.

The name *sheela-na-gig* comes from the Irish language, but its meaning and origin are uncertain. It may originally have been *síle na gcíoch*, taken to mean "woman of the breasts," or *síle-ina-giob*, meaning "an old woman on her hunkers," from the unusual squatting position of the figure. She is also known by a number of other names—Giddy

Julia, St. Shanahan, the Castle Hag, Sheila O'Dwyer, or the Devil Stone or Devil Woman, to list a few. She is depicted as a very small, very old woman, completely naked, crouching down with her thin arms wrapped round her knees. Her ribs sometimes show in an emaciated body, and in some carvings she seems to be completely bald.

Sheela-Na-Gigs and Churches

Generally speaking, representations of sheela-na-gigs are to be found within churches and castles, and assume a close connection with these buildings. This is reminiscent of some leprechauns who, as we saw earlier, make their homes in ruined abbeys and abandoned houses. The name *sheela-na-gig* was first used in the Proceedings of the Royal Irish Academy, 1840–1844, to describe the strange carved creature found on the gable wall of a church at Rochestown, County Tipperary. The name was also used in 1840 by John O'Donovan, official of the Ordnance Survey, to describe a similar carved figure on the wall of Kiltinane Church (also in Tipperary). Many other similar carvings are found in churches and great houses scattered throughout Ireland, showing the demographic spread of the tiny beings.

Neither Irish history nor folklore records what manner of creature is so depicted or how she came to be incorporated in medieval Irish sculpture. Many people throughout Ireland believe that she may have been some sort of early fairy.

Rúairí O'Tunney

There is an old legend concerning a stonemason named Rúairí O'Tunney, from the Kilkenny area, who was the finest mason of his day and who founded an entire Irish school of funerary monument design in the late fifteenth or early sixteenth century. He was allegedly taught all his skills by an extremely ancient female fairy creature, whom he rewarded by placing her image all over Ireland, in his own work and in the work of his pupils. His style and imagery were copied by the later Ormond ornamental school, founded by one of the Butler earls of Ormond in the 1600s. Might this "elderly female fairy" who instructed the stonemason have been a sheela-na-gig, a sort of female leprechaun?

In counties Cavan and Westmeath, these female creatures seem to have been quite ferocious; local representations of them show them to have teeth. A fanged being watches over a low gateway at the back of the castle in Moate, County Westmeath, set into an old wall that is thought to have been built around 1649. Similar carvings are to be seen at Lavey (County Cavan), Clonmel (County Tipperary) and Ballyporty (County Clare). Might these have been guardians of the buildings, just as the cluricaun was regarded as a guardian in some more lowly Irish houses?

Certainly, such entities seem to provide a tangible connection between the medieval Christian world and the earlier pagan existence. These elderly leprechaun-like fairies may very well date from long before Christianity arrived in Ireland. One of the most ancient of these carved figures comes from Seir Kieran in County Offaly; it is carved in a monastic enclosure, which, in turn, was built upon the site of an extremely early Christian settlement (dated to as far back as C.E. 401—thirty or so years before Patrick's arrival in Ireland). The carving was on the east gable of the Church of Ireland there, and its pagan presence so offended one of the clergy that he had it removed and sent to the National Museum of Ireland in Dublin.

The Church may still be very uneasy about the close proximity of such fairy beings; it is said to have regarded them with some degree of abhorrence, but it nevertheless allowed them to be brought within its precincts and incorporated into its designs so that the holy influence of the site might either limit or extinguish their dark and evil powers.

Sheela-Na-Gigs and Leprechauns

Leprechauns, of course, with their usual disdain, claim that sheela-na-gigs have never had anything to do with them, even in the remote and distant past. There never have been any females of their species whatsoever, they declare (thereby giving us our only clue to their origins). The carvings, leprechauns go on to say, are nothing more than creations of the medieval mind and have more to do with humans than with fairies. Why else, they ask, would they be turning up in active Christian churches, where no leprechaun (let alone a fairy) would ever go?

And yet, even leprechauns appear to be a little afraid of the stone carvings; leprechauns are known to treat the relics with extreme reverence and respect when they encounter them in old ruins. Perhaps there is more of a connection between the two than we suspect.

CHAPTER 17

LEPRECHAUNS IN POPULAR CULTURE

During the late twentieth and early twenty-first centuries, the world began to change and continues to do so today. Technological innovation, new forms of medicine, revolution in communication, more "science-based" beliefs, and increasing urbanization have all led to both the decline and in some cases the eradication of old folk-based and communal ways of looking at the world. Large areas of open countryside, shadowy woodlands, hidden lakes and secret marshes have all disappeared under urban expansion and countryside developments. The communal gatherings that often characterized the rural environment have now been replaced by television, iPads, smartphones, and tablets, and areas once closely knit are drifting further and further apart.

Rather than depending on folk traditions, most people now consult formal medicine, technology, and social services. Folklore and folkways are starting to die out in many respects and the way mankind lives now is very different from that of a hundred years ago. And so are the belief systems of the populace—where once many were ready to believe in curses, witchcraft, and fairies as a means of explanation of events, now there is a greater tendency to look for a scientific reason. Consequently, fairies have often given way to technological phenomena and discourse. Rather than looking for "little green men" in the hedgerows, we are now more likely to believe we can find them on the surface of Mars.

Leprechauns and the Modern World

Given this constant change and fluid nature of society, how well has the leprechaun fared in the modern world? The answer is a complex one: he has and he hasn't. While belief in him as a fairy has certainly declined, he has proved more adaptable than other fairies who have faded away into the Celtic Twilight, by simply changing aspects of his personality to fit with the perceptions of the developing Western world. Rather than being "just another fairy," he has subtly adapted himself to become identified with the spirit of Ireland itself, and thus has skillfully positioned himself to be ingrained into the advancing technological society. All the same, the onset of the twenty-first century has proved difficult for the leprechaun population in general.

Social Urbanization

One of the characteristics of modern society is its increasing urban expansion. What were once small towns, villages and hamlets are finding themselves under new development with house-building and the provision of modern resources and facilities—shops, factories, housing estates—on the increase. Farming, too, is expanding and becoming part of growing industrialized areas focused on mass production. Consequently, much of the ancient landscape is disappearing and with it the habitat of many fairies including the leprechaun.

Traditionally, the leprechaun was to be found hidden away under hedges and bushes along gullies and ditches, which masked him from human gaze as he went about his business. He made his home in old raths and ancient tumuli dotted about the countryside. These, however, are rapidly disappearing under shopping malls, industrial centers, road networks, and general housing. Fairy mounds and lone trees (said to be *skeaghs* or "fairy trees") are being swept away by new developments or farming programs. At one time, to remove one of these would have been considered a desecration and would invite grim retribution from the fairy folk, but not anymore.

A LEPRECHAUN COLONY

There is an existing leprechaun colony in Portland, Oregon, but only a few can see it. It was discovered in 1975, when a local man noticed a strange hole at the bottom of a streetlight. It became an official park in 1976, and visitors have brought tiny additions to it.

The result is that the leprechaun has had to react to the increasing urban sprawl. Some folklorists argue that urbanization has led to a decrease in leprechaun numbers and that their reproduction (however it comes about) has slowed. Leprechauns, they argue, are like the African white rhino and on the edge of extinction. However, this is only one viewpoint. It has also been contended that despite certain accounts of great gatherings, leprechauns only made up a small part of Irish fairydom and never existed in massive numbers in any case. Because of their secretiveness, cunning, and surly disposition, leprechaun demographic patterns, it is argued, are extremely difficult to ascertain. There is a further confusion with other types of fairies, like brollachans, glaistigs, and redcaps, who have perhaps migrated from Scotland or elsewhere and can sometimes be classed as leprechauns, thus distorting the picture. Since these entities are extremely dangerous (a brollachan can in some instances possess an unwary human), little research has been done on them and they are simply lumped together as "leprechauns" when they are not. This makes it impossible to estimate the impact of urbanization on leprechaun numbers.

Adaptability

Further, as the leprechaun is both crafty and highly adaptable, it is possible (indeed highly probable) that they have integrated themselves into urban communities. Although their natural environment is the countryside (and it is this environment with which they are mostly associated), they can find urban areas in which to make a home and a living.

They may, for example, be found under old culverts and drains or in abandoned or derelict buildings within urban areas. Disused public houses, for example, are especially attractive, since the jollity of former days, coupled with the fumes of long-vanished alcohol trapped in the stonework, are alluring to the leprechaun. However, they also are known to settle in other deserted buildings (with the exception of abandoned churches); the noises of their comings and goings often lead to the suggestion that these places are "haunted." As a generalization, then, it is believed that while eschewing the more modern aspects of town and city centers, the leprechaun seeks out rundown and dilapidated urban centers in order to make his home.

But it is drains and culverts that most attract city-living leprechauns, especially those that are tucked away in shadowy corners of the city. Some of these, of course, can be conduits for interconnecting power cables, and it is here that the leprechaun can have an effect on the efficient running of the urban environment. Some leprechauns have adapted themselves to using modern power. In the old days, they may have cooked their meals over tiny fires or worked by the light of the moon or a candle; nowadays, they are more likely to use modern power for their needs. Certain of them, it would seem, have become skilled electricians. This may not seem so unusual since, as fairy shoemakers, leprechauns are well-accustomed to intricate work requiring intense concentration. Therefore, it may be common for him to work with small cables and connectors and use them to set up diversions in the urban power system. This may of course create problems for other urban-dwellers as small communities of leprechauns within a certain area "leech" power from the main grid for their own purposes, creating glitches in the system. This may lead to dips in power in homes, factories and other facilities. Some users in certain areas have also reported similar glitches in the telephone system which may originate in the same way.

Leprechaun Pranks

Leprechauns can also become nuisances in built-up areas. They play pranks on householders, just as they do on the country cottagers, except in the modern home there is much more to play with. So instead of simply hiding things or breaking crockery, they can cause electrical equipment to fail, washing machines to flood, and temperatures in fridges to fluctuate, destroying food in the process. They can also cause computers, smartphones, and tablets to fail or display the wrong messages. In a wider sense, they can cause disruption to traffic lights, burglar alarms, and cable TV, often providing a cover for many of their activities. They are probably responsible for many of the "pranks" that blight some communities, which are often blamed on irresponsible youth. It may be a good idea to think twice before apportioning blame—such problems may be very well down to leprechauns who have never truly settled within an urban environment and who really can't get along with their human neighbors.

Leprechauns As Irish Icons

In an era in which image is everything, leprechauns have successfully adopted this philosophy and ensured their place in the public mind. They have also been willing to travel outside of Ireland to ensure this image is more widely known. The only other fairy to achieve similar iconic recognition is the banshee. Many fairies tend to be restricted to a particular place or location. Not so the leprechaun. Like the banshee, he has followed the Irish diaspora to other parts of the world, and he has done this by making himself the very symbol of Ireland in the popular mind.

LEPRECHAUN TRAPS

In recent years, several companies have manufactured "leprechaun traps." These usually consist of a bright, shiny, coin-like object placed on a pressure plate below a drop-container. It relies on the leprechaun's greed and curiosity to be effective. However, the wily leprechauns have ensured that they are usually ineffective.

Trading on his reputation as a land spirit, the leprechaun has turned himself into the physical embodiment of the land itself, a move that has endeared him both to the Irish living at home and those who have traveled abroad and are nostalgic for their homeland. Sine the leprechaun is an earth spirit, this transition has not proved all that difficult; he has adopted Irish country mannerisms (for example, he has taken to leaning on a *shillelagh*—a stout blackthorn stick—or smoking a dudeen or cob pipe) and has sometimes adopted the green and verdant color of the countryside. The little man in the green suit, as he is portrayed (and remember, very few leprechauns wear green suits. Most wear mismatched and multicolored clothing), has become the very symbol of Ireland, particularly for those who are living in other countries or are of Irish origin. In this, the leprechaun has become a master of PR, almost turning himself into a brand name. This may arise because more than any other fairy (with perhaps the exception of the banshee, and even *her* ability to adapt seems a bit limited), the leprechaun has embraced modern thinking and has seen how to meet modern—particularly Irish—needs. With an innate and unfailing knowledge of his market, he has found a way to appeal to the romantic, nostalgic, and whimsical side of the Irish. Thus, when Irish folk in public houses in Kilburn and New York raise a glass to "the oul' sod" (i.e., Ireland) it is the leprechaun they are thinking about in his role as a symbol of the Irish landscape.

The False Image

In conjunction with this revised image, the leprechaun likes to give the impression that he's a jolly little fellow, a charming rogue with a silver tongue who is a friend to all (especially those who are buying strong drink). This perception endears him to many people, not only the Irish, making him a loveable, if rather rakish, character. However,

PART III: HOW DO LEPRECHAUNS LIVE?

as we already know, leprechauns are for the most part far from jolly or even friendly beings—they are at best moody and at worst hostile—and the impression of jocularity that they create is little more than a PR exercise. But it has certainly worked, and the leprechaun is generally thought of as a wisecracking and merry imp, supposedly representative of the Irish themselves, and this has ensured their position as worldwide representatives of Ireland. Thus, far from being a "local fairy" the leprechaun has become an international figure, recognized in many countries but chiefly in America. The reason for this American popularity—which is unrivaled anywhere outside of Ireland itself—is that during the mid-nineteenth century, as the Irish Potato Famine ravaged Ireland, many families fled the deprivations of the country to the shores of America. There, life was said to be considerably better. These families took many of their beliefs and stories with them, and the leprechaun ensured that his stories were among them. Of course, it helped that some of the indigenous peoples had similar stories of "little people" (the Choctaw Indians, for example, called them Kwanokasha and greatly feared them) into which the leprechauns could meld and so continue their own traditions. Many of these stories became intertwined, and a corpus of lore concerning small fairies, which included the leprechaun, was built up in the United States. Therefore, in many people's minds (perhaps not only in Ireland and America but elsewhere as well), the leprechaun has skillfully made himself synonymous with the land of his birth.

Leprechauns in Advertising and Promotion

Much of modern society is based on consumerism. We are continually being bombarded with advertisements designed to encourage us to buy certain goods or services, and indeed this has become a part of modern life. The crafty leprechaun realizes this. We have already discussed how he has become the symbol of Ireland to many people around the world and how he has cultivated the image of himself as a lovable rogue. Taking this a step further, he has adapted his image to align with various consumer items that appear in advertising. Having made himself a brand image for Ireland, he can also extend this into the commercial market and perhaps make himself some money. (Leprechauns are always on the lookout for ways of increasing their personal fortune, which they do not spend of course.)

It is suspected, therefore that leprechauns have secretly entered into commercial agreements with a number of companies of various kinds to promote their products through the fairy's image. Because the leprechaun is now such a well-known figure in many parts of the world, this is somewhat akin to contracting a famous sportsperson or Hollywood actor to promote the product. It is not known whether the contract is made directly with the leprechaun or through an agent; however, it is thought that such contracts are incredibly lucrative and add immensely to the leprechaun's treasure. In some cases, the companies involved may not know they are dealing with leprechauns as business partners; the executives are often forced to sign non-disclosure agreements to prevent them from revealing the identities of their colleagues (the leprechaun enjoys his anonymity).

Leprechaun Fabric and Pottery

Many of the companies with whom leprechauns deal are manufacturers of fabrics—though some leprechauns have been known to extend their commercial portfolios to deal with potters and ceramic manufacturers. Such companies seem to be their preferred options. Thus, we find leprechaun images on towels, tea towels, handkerchiefs, and even T-shirts. We also find him on teapots and knickknacks. Souvenir shops, particularly in Ireland, are bursting with items bearing the image, some of them made under fairy licenses. Walk into a number of airport gift shops in places like Dublin, Cork, or even Belfast, and a hundred of the little fellows in green suits look back at you.

But it is not only fabric and clothing manufacturers who have taken the leprechaun as their advertising mascot. Some food manufacturers, too, have adopted the symbol of the fairy as part of the marketing (though probably not under license from the fairy itself) to promote their wares. The most famous of such images is perhaps Lucky the Leprechaun, the advertising image of Lucky Charms breakfast cereal, produced by the General Mills food company (GM) since 1964. It consists of toasted oats and multicolored marshmallow pieces and is hugely popular not only in the United States but also around the world.

Lucky the Leprechaun

Lucky is not covered by leprechaun image rights registered to the fairy world, or course, but was the creation of advertising writer Pat McInroy and GM's creative director Tony Jaffe, who worked for what is now the advertising agency Saatchi & Saatchi. This advertising strategy drew on the already established popularity of the leprechaun in the public mind. Although Lucky has been created by humans, the image must have had leprechaun approval since the cereal was such a widespread success. Indeed, Americans took Lucky into their hearts. He featured in animated TV commercials, in full-color advertising displays, and even in comics—both in ordinary comic books and in the Sunday newspaper comic sections! The leprechauns still must have approved.

> ## HONORARY LEPRECHAUNS
> With today's growing commercialism, some communities (especially Irish majority ones) across the US have declared "Leprechaun Days," when various festivities are organized and leprechaun memorabilia is sold. This usually happens around St. Patrick's Day, and individuals can apply to become "honorary leprechauns" for the day. It's not known whether the leprechauns approve or not.

Just to demonstrate this, seven years after he first appeared, there was an attempt to introduce a new marketing image by the company. This was Waldo the Wizard who appeared on the Lucky Charms boxes. He was a kindly, absent-minded character in a flowing cloak and a wizard hat. His selling point was that he was always looking for a box of Lucky Charms which he had mislaid. He was created in 1975 by Alan Snedeker of the same advertising agency that had created Lucky with a catchphrase which declared that the cereal was "ibbldebibblede-licious." He was tested on audiences in New England and apparently "beat Lucky hands down" and so looked set to take over as the new face of Lucky Charms. However, the change of promotional image must not have pleased the leprechauns for Waldo lasted less than a year.

According to some sources, sales began to plummet as customers turned to other cereals and while a hit in parts of New England,

Waldo never really took off in the rest of the United States. He was quietly withdrawn in 1976, and now exists only in the General Mills archives. Lucky returned in great triumph and adapted some of Waldo's selling points to enhance his own reputation as a commercial image. Indeed, at one time he was one of the best-known advertising symbols in America. It might be stretching a point to say that the leprechauns themselves objected to the introduction of Waldo as the main image of the cereal and that they in some way contributed to his rather ignominious end, but perhaps one cannot help but wonder.

Leprechauns and Drink

Leprechauns have always been associated with drink—elsewhere in this book we mentioned their prowess as distillers. Surely some enterprising human distiller would take the leprechaun motif and use it to promote their spirit product. Certainly, the Irish distiller Malcolm Brown based in Dundalk, Ireland was not slow in this respect with its Flaming Leprechaun Whiskey, which began to expand into other distinctly unIrish spirits—gin, rum, vodka, etc. On the label of the whiskey bottles is the figure of a leprechaun wearing a crown (to represent the King of the Fairies), and this undoubtedly appeals to the leprechauns' vanity (although they are distillers and shoemakers, they still consider themselves to be very important in the fairy world). Maybe less acceptable are other images on other spirit bottles showing the leprechaun as a pirate (rum), as a Russian (vodka), and alarmingly, wearing an English-style hat (gin)! However, such is the leprechauns' love of spirits of any type that they take all this in good part, and as long as their race is prominently featured on the label they are willing to let it go. Recently, in 2016, Flaming Leprechaun announced a partnership with United Liquors, the US's seventh-largest distributor, which gives an indication that the leprechauns approve, or at least are tolerant, of their portrayal by the company. And, from time to time, other distillers and brewers have also used the leprechaun motif on the labels of their products usually without any objection from the fairy world. However, most of these have been "specials," which are available usually around festivals such as St. Patrick's Day.

Sports

The leprechaun has not only represented the food and drink industries but, curiously, sports organizations as well. Most notably, he is the mascot of the Boston Celtics basketball team, which is are part of the National Basketball Association Eastern Conference Atlantic Division. The Celtics were founded in 1946 and play at the TD Garden in Boston. The name probably reflects the number of Irish people living in the city at the time of its founding. Not only is the leprechaun their physical mascot, but he also appears on all their advertising—his name, coincidentally, is Lucky, although he's not connected to the leprechaun who advertises Lucky Charms breakfast cereal. Indeed, the leprechaun motif has only been adopted in its present form since the 1970s. Nevertheless, the leprechaun was associated with the Celtics since the 1950s, when a representation of the fairy was designed by the brother of then Celtics coach, Arnold "Red" Auerbach.

The fairy who appears on the Celtics promotional material is a rather dapperly dressed figure in a smart shamrock waistcoat, a green bow tie, and a ribboned hat, his outfit complete with shiny buckled shoes—unlike the untidily dressed Irish folklore leprechaun—leaning on a shillelagh, winking an eye and spinning a ball on his forefinger. He is easily recognizable.

However, the idea of a mascot who appears at Celtics games and is played by a real person, poses some problems in the leprechaun world. First, a *human* is dressed as one of their own. This could irritate some leprechauns, who consider themselves to be far superior to mortals. Second, this places the fairy in the same realm as some of the other basketball team mascots, such as Hugo the Hornet (the Charlotte Hornets), the Jazz Bear (Utah Jazz) or even Stuff the Magic Dragon (Orlando Magic), which some leprechauns may find demeaning to their species. Perhaps as a result of this, the person who played the mascot Lucky the Leprechaun has sometimes found himself in difficult circumstances from time to time with the company that owns the team. For instance, in 2009, Damon Lee Blust, a skilled gymnast who appeared as Lucky, was "relieved of his contract" for failing to turn up for promotional and charity appearances. Could it have been that the whole affair was engineered by leprechauns who might have taken exception to his portrayal of Lucky? Perhaps not, but it is maybe something worth considering. Advertisers and promoters would need to be on their guard!

SHILLELAGH
A shillelagh is a blackthorn walking stick that doubles as a club during disputes between the Irish. It is strong with a large wooden knob on top.

Leprechauns in Film and Exhibition

It should come as no surprise that with all the folklore that surrounds him and his inherent connections with Ireland, the leprechaun should feature in modern films. A mistake that he is a lovable and humorous character has greatly aided his transition from folktale to the big screen. There is also the nostalgia element in the character, which makes him appeal to those Irish who are watching these films in faraway places and dreaming of their home country. The tourist's Ireland is, of course, a mystical country that bears no resemblance to the real place—a region in which leprechauns are regularly seen. Roughly speaking, leprechauns began to regularly appear in movies sometime around the late 1950s and early 1960s (although the Henry Koster movie *The Luck of the Irish*, released in 1948 and starring Tyrone Power and Jayne Meadows, had featured a leprechaun among its characters), and were often sentimental in their tone.

One of the earliest movies to cash in on this misty-eyed Irish nostalgia—described today as "paddywhackery" (fake) by some critics—was Robert Stevenson's 1959 film *Darby O'Gill and the Little People*, which starred Sean Connery and Janet Munro as well as Jimmy O'Dea as Brian, self-styled king of the Leprechauns. The film, released by Walt Disney Productions, was based on two books: *Darby O'Gill and the Good People* and *The Ashes of Old Wishes and Other Darby O'Gill Tales* by Herminie Templeton Kavanagh (who had been born in County Longford, Ireland). Part of the film focused on Darby O'Gill, the aging caretaker of Lord Fitzpatrick's estate, and his attempts to catch leprechauns, who always managed to outwit him. The film was a mishmash of Irish folklore (including the banshee and the *cóiste bodhar* or "death coach"), romance, and sentiment, and was a terrific hit, especially in the United States. Its "Irishness" appealed to many audiences, as did the cast (especially O'Dea), although some critics described Connery (who went on to star in the James Bond franchise and many other movies) as "rather wooden." But *Darby* was generally considered "a classic" and made a great deal of money for its producers. Even today, it is still shown on television around Christmas or Easter.

Finian's Rainbow

Following the same Irish nostalgia, Warner Brothers subsequently released *Finian's Rainbow* in 1968. This was a musical starring Fred Astaire and Petula Clark, based on the stage musical of the same name. It has the distinction of being directed by Francis Ford Coppola, who went on to direct such movies as *The Godfather*, *Apocalypse Now*, and *The Cotton Club*. It centered on the premise that every leprechaun has a crock of gold buried at the end of a rainbow. This, of course, is wrong; the wily leprechaun does not keep all his money in one place, but has it scattered in a number of different locations. It also seems to suggest that if the leprechaun loses the crock, he will turn into a human. This is not folkloric either; however, it is known that if a leprechaun loses money in any way, he will stop at nothing until he gets it back. The leprechaun in the film was played by British rock 'n' roll singer Tommy Steele and was known by the name of Og (which made him sound like a prehistoric caveman).

Finian's Rainbow was released at a time when movie musicals were on the wane, which initially led to rather dismissive critical reviews. All the same, it was a reasonable hit across America and was nominated for a Golden Globe Award. In all these films, the leprechaun is projected as the "spirit of oul' Ireland," a mischievous but basically good-hearted rogue. Probably because of this, the leprechauns have taken no great exception to their portrayal in these films. And quite possibly, always having an ear for a good tune, they enjoyed the music in *Finian's Rainbow* and were prepared to overlook any other inconsistencies about themselves.

Leprechaun

However, although he is often portrayed as a "jolly little fellow," the leprechaun as we have seen has a much darker side. Recognizing this, director Mark Jones decided to develop a malignant leprechaun as part of the horror film genre. This he did in the film *Leprechaun*, which went on general release through Trimark Pictures in 1993 and starred a very young Jennifer Aniston. Once again it featured a leprechaun (this time a murderous one) protecting his crock of gold. Although Jones had intended the leprechaun to be a dark, psychopathic creature, it didn't work out that way. The fairy was played by English actor Warwick Davis, who went on to feature in Star Wars and Harry Potter and who brought an edge of dark humor to the part. Unfortunately, the movie was up against some very stiff competition at the box office—this was a year of major movie releases: *The Fugitive*, *Jurassic Park*, and *Mrs. Doubtfire*—and while it was moderately popular, it was not a financial success. However, it was successful enough for *Leprechaun 2* to make an appearance in cinemas.

This film, directed by Rodman Flender, portrayed the leprechaun (Davis again) as an even more sadistic and remorseless creature. In essence, it was a "slasher movie." It also introduced the idea of a leprechaun being destroyed by wrought iron (the protagonist is "killed" by having an iron crowbar rammed into his chest like a vampire). Considering that the leprechauns are often metalworkers themselves, the idea of iron (wrought or otherwise) holds no terrors for them.

Indeed, it's possible that the leprechaun community took exception to this film as it was a complete flop at the box office and became the last of the Leprechaun horror film to be released in theaters. All the other films in what became known as the "Leprechaun series"—*Leprechauns 3* and *4*; *Leprechaun in Space*; *Leprechaun in the Hood 1* and *2*; and *Leprechaun: Origins*—were all released straight to video and in many cases were panned by the critics.

Davis appeared as the leprechaun in all the movies except the final offering, when his part was taken by former wrestler Dylan Postl. There is some talk of another Leprechaun movie being released in 2019 and being aired on Syfy, but if this happens, presumably the director will seek the approval of the leprechaun community.

LEPRECHAUNISM

There is a rare genetic condition known as "leprechaunism" (Donohue syndrome), which is partly caused by the body's abnormal resistance to insulin. It affects the endocrine system, which regulates hormones in the blood. Symptoms include low-set ears, a flat nose with upturned nostrils, low body fat, and possible excessive hair growth.

Along with the original film, Trimark Studios released an eight-page comic as a kind of prequel. The plot of the comic bore no relation to the film, and therefore did not sell well. However, the comic angle on the leprechaun was far from finished. In 2009, Bluewater Productions (now TidalWave Productions) of Vancouver, Washington, launched a *Leprechaun* comic title, written by Zach Hunchar and drawn by Kris Carter. The comic lasted only four issues and then was abruptly canceled. At the same time, Marvel Comics was also believed to be negotiating to include the leprechaun figure in its *Warlock* series, but this did not come to fruition. Obviously, the leprechaun species does not approve of being depicted in comic books, which its members may feel demeans them as a race.

Although they resist being associated with certain films and comic books, the leprechauns do not seem averse to promotion through displays and exhibitions. A number of towns and villages throughout Ireland play host to "leprechaun parades," particularly around St. Patrick's Day. These often include displays and sales of things such as "fairy butter" (attributed to the leprechauns) or "leprechaun bread" in the style of a farmer's market. And the idea goes even further—in Dublin, the National Leprechaun Museum of Ireland has opened its doors, displaying all things leprechaun, and is one of the city's major tourist attractions, with a gift shop containing many representations of this particular fairy.

A Fairy Cavern

It is not only Dublin that has a leprechaun visitor attraction. The Liberties of Carlingford in County Louth boast a "fairy cavern." According to local folklore, in 1989, a leprechaun suit with four small gold coins in the pocket and the bones of a little man were found on Slieve Foy mountain, just above Carlingford. The man who found them—local pub owner P.J. O'Hare—placed the suit in a glass case in his pub. No one knows what became of the coins. One of P.J.'s friends, Kevin Woods (known locally as "McCoiltte"), went onto the mountain determined to disprove the story. Instead, he encountered a leprechaun with whom he found he could communicate.

The leprechaun, who gave his name as Carraig, stated that he was one of 236 remaining leprechauns and that his race was dying out in Ireland. Once there had been millions of his kind, but people had stopped believing in them and they began to disappear. McCoiltte published the story of the leprechauns in a book, *The Last Leprechauns of Ireland*, which he used to gain them protected status under European Union legislation in 2009. Shortly after, he started a series of "leprechaun hunts" in the surrounding countryside, similar to treasure hunts, wherein participants had to find 100 ceramic leprechauns hiding 2,000 euros. These hunts occur when the clocks go forward for British Summer Time, and are still popular today.

Not only this but McCoiltte has obtained European money to develop a "fairy cavern" from an old leprechaun house with tunnels going back and forth from other locations including the Fairy Glen near Rostrevor in County Down. McCoiltte, who is charge of the cavern (another tourist attraction in the area), styles himself as "Ireland's Last Leprechaun Whisperer" and claims he speaks to the fairies of the area on a regular basis. There is no doubt that this is an attractive center for tourists (particularly from the US) and that it clearly has the blessing (as does the National Leprechaun Museum in Dublin) of the leprechauns themselves, since such attractions show their importance and display them in a good light. However, there are other people who claim to communicate with leprechauns and occasionally give lectures on the subject to tourists. For instance, a man named McPoland who lived in the Mourne Mountains of County Down made a reasonable living speaking on the subject to visitors and acting as a guide. He claimed he had found a bag of about six golden coins wedged in a drystone mountain wall (which later conveniently vanished) and this gave him the power to see and talk to the leprechauns. However, the fairies may not have taken to him because his tourist business was not a success and eventually folded. They can always spot an opportunist!

Into the Future

Despite being often seen as "folksy sprites of a former time," leprechauns have by contrast adapted well to the modern world. In fact, the leprechaun has managed to push himself forward in the public consciousness both as a national icon and as a money-making promotional figure in a rapidly changing and media-orientated world.

And what of the future? As the world becomes more and more computerized, as international travel becomes the order of the day, and as people become increasingly materialistic and skeptical, can the leprechaun survive both as an idea and a species? Maybe not, but I wouldn't bet against it!

CONCLUSION

Far from being simply an iconic representation of Ireland, the leprechaun is an extremely complex and contradictory being, to whom no amount of words will do justice. He is not a jolly and irrepressible cobbler—the stereotyped image by which he is usually portrayed. Leprechauns, as has hopefully been shown in this book, are surly and evasive creatures who will do mortals a bad turn just as quickly as a good one. They are frequently drunken and miserly, and even shun the company of other supernatural beings.

Leprechauns belong to a class of diminutive creatures that exist right across the world. They are related to the kobolds, the rock-trolls and other entities which live under the earth, which appear in the folklore of many nations. In England, for example, the leprechaun appears as Robin Goodfellow or Lob Lie-by-the-fire. In Wales, he appears as the *bwca* or brownie. In Germany, he is known as a hobgoblin—a little fellow who dwells by the hearth and who must be placated by members of the household. Among the Native Americans, as in Ireland, leprechaun-creatures are known as "the little people of the mounds." Perhaps, as we have suggested, there may be connections between them all.

Do leprechauns actually exist? Maybe they are the final vestige of some distant race or smaller species that once coexisted with mankind. Maybe they are a vague recollection of ancient and powerful gods worshipped in some prehistoric time, whose stature has gradually diminished over the generations. Or maybe they are out there, lurking among the bushes and hedgerows of Ireland, waiting to play a trick or do some mischief.

CONCLUSION

Whether or not they are out there, leprechauns hold a powerful fascination for the Irish imagination (and that of other races as well). Despite their disagreeable ways and grudging attitude, there is something within their nature that sets them apart from other "little folk" and that is attractive to the human psyche.

Since, when you think about it, leprechauns have much to commend them.

Leprechauns are often unwashed and scruffy, but in an age where "image is everything" and mortals are frequently judged on the way they look rather than on what is in their hearts, leprechauns show a refreshing absence of personal vanity.

They are careful with their money—which, when properly considered, is no great vice. Certainly they have a tremendous love for gold, but unlike mortals, they do not despoil the environment to get at it. Indeed, they are the self-appointed guardians of the earth, taking revenge upon those who do it harm. In an age when natural things take a poor second place to capitalism and material expansion (which are often styled as "development"), it is good to know that at least *someone* is keeping an eye on our world—even if it is not us.

Leprechauns are the embodiment of the landscape, providing a sense of continuity from one era to the next. In an age when everything is transient, this is not a bad thing. They provide a link between our own bustling reality and the more leisurely era of our forefathers—a sense of history and place. In a world where values are fast disappearing and time is master of us all, the leprechauns' approach to life is a thing to be treasured and nurtured.

The leprechaun, then, is more than a simple symbol of Ireland on a postcard, cup, or tea cloth. He is the representation of the deeper truths which often lie hidden—like the leprechaun himself—in the secret places of the Irish mind and heart.

INDEX

Abbeys, 31–36, 190
Abductions, 18–20, 58
Advertising images, 201–5
Ahern, Kate, 153
Allingham, William, 5, 29
Anderson, Tommy, 92–93
Aniston, Jennifer, 209
Art, 132
The Ashes of Old Wishes and Other Darby O'Gill Tales, 207
Astaire, Fred, 208
Au Pays des Pardons, 75
Auerbach, Arnold "Red," 205

Bachall, 143–44, 146
Bankers, 117–25
Banshees, 15, 35, 59, 67, 104–5, 166, 198–99, 207
Baptisms, 18–20, 61–65, 152
Beltane Fair, 81, 108
Blacksmiths, 94–96
Blust, Damon Lee, 206
Bodhrán, 113
Boru, Brian, 59, 81–83, 95
Bradley, Peggy, 93
Braz, Anatole le, 75
Brighid, 105–6
Brownies, 11–12, 38, 69–72, 92–94, 177–78, 215
Buí, Cathal, 136
Builders, 91–94

Campbell, J.G., 33
Candlemas Day, 105
Carter, Kris, 210
Carvings, 190–92
Castles, 32–35, 49, 133–34, 172–78, 190–91
Cecil, Douglas, 176
Céilís, 42–43, 89–90, 98–99, 102–9, 114–15, 162
Changelings, 58
Chessmen, 38–39
Chiefs, 138–40, 181
Christmas, 107, 208
Churches, 31–36, 59–65, 147–58, 164–68, 190–91
Clans, 129–40
Clark, Petula, 208
Clothing, 24–27, 131, 136, 184, 199, 202
Cluricauns
    appearance of, 184–85
    characteristics of, 185–89
    as drinkers, 185–86
    leprechauns and, 136, 183–84, 188–91
    as storytellers, 186–87
    temperament of, 185–89
Cobblers, 13, 26, 89, 94, 125, 163, 215. *See also* Shoemakers
Colfer, Eoin, 25
Colors, favorite, 26–27

INDEX

Complexion, 60, 67
Connaught leprechauns, 108, 130, 132–33, 139–42, 184, 188
Connery, Sean, 35, 207
Coppola, Francis Ford, 208
Craig, Frank, 171, 172, 176
Crom Dubh's Day, 107
Cromwell, Oliver, 80

Dancing, 42–43, 89–90, 98–99, 102–9, 114–15, 186
"Danny Boy," 97
Darby O'Gill and the Good People, 207
Darby O'Gill and the Little People, 35, 207
Davis, Warwick, 209–10
Dead
   exorcisms and, 153–59, 164
   feast of, 161
   freeing, 164–65
   funerals for, 161–64
   power over, 165–68
Demons, 67, 147–48, 153–56, 180
Devil, 64, 125, 148–50, 153–56, 159, 190
Distillers, 48–49, 105, 108, 111–12, 145, 204–5
"Don't Copy Leprechaun Music," 98–101
Drums, 113
Dudeens/pipes, 27, 41, 58, 184, 186, 199
Dullahan, 15, 67
Dwarves, 10, 59, 168, 180–82
"Dwellers of the mounds," 5–6, 215. *See also* Fairy mounds
Dwellings, 5–6, 31–40, 91–94, 215

Eilean Mor, 33
Elizabeth I, Queen, 178
Elves, 12, 15
Entertainment, 97–109, 111–16

Evil deeds, 14, 75–77, 107–8, 147–59, 164–65, 192
Evil forces, 18, 64, 147, 164–65, 192
Evil spirits, 19, 77, 104, 147, 153, 168, 187
Evil tricks, 5, 16, 164–65
Exhibitions/displays, 211–12
Exorcisms, 153–59, 164

Fabrics, 202
Fáilte na Marbh, 161
Fairies. *See also* Leprechauns
   characteristics of, 5–6, 10–14
   description of, 5–6, 9–21
   lifestyles of, 10–11, 68–69, 127–216
   overview of, 5–6, 9–21
   solitary fairies, 14–15, 33–34, 55, 67, 72–77, 83–84, 102–3, 109, 129, 179–81
   temperament of, 10–14
   trooping fairies, 13–14, 37, 51, 68, 89, 103–4, 115, 118
"The Fairies," 5
Fairs, 81, 95, 102–9, 137, 142. *See also* Festivals
Fairy bankers, 117–25
Fairy cavalcade, 13–14, 37, 89, 103–4, 115, 162
Fairy cavern, 211–12
Fairy child, 57–64
Fairy fights, 140
Fairy funerals, 161–64
Fairy horses, 96
"The Fairy Mother," 59–64
Fairy mounds, 10, 14, 18–21, 65–69, 89, 169, 195
"The Fairy of Kintail," 76–77
Fairy-human unions, 59
Famine, 91, 108, 200
Feast of the Dead, 161
Fées, 9, 11, 56, 73–75

– 218 –

INDEX

Female creatures, 32–34, 55–58, 69–77, 189–92
Ferganainm, 138–40
Festivals, 81, 97, 102–9, 139–40, 165, 205, 211. *See also* Fairs
Films, 206–10
Finian's Rainbow, 208
"The Fishermen and the Fairies," 34–35
Fitzpatrick, W.J., 39–40, 148
Flender, Rodman, 209
Funerals, 161–64

Gallagher, Margaret, 162
Gallagher, Pat, 162–64
Gender, 55–77
Gerald of Wales, 98
Ghost stories, 114–15
Ghosts, 67, 95, 105, 113–15, 147, 154–55, 165–68, 187
"The Girl Who Stayed Too Long," 41–46
Glaistigs, 32–33, 72–73
Gnomes, 11, 20, 179
Goblins, 11, 19, 35, 94–95, 137, 215
Gold, guarding, 117–25
Gold, hoarding, 118–24, 186, 208–9
"Grand Himself," 138–40
Greatrakes, Valentine, 158
Grogochs, 11, 37, 56, 69–73, 85, 132, 169–79
Gruagach, 69–71

Hair color, 66–67
Halfling, 66
Halloween, 14, 103–5, 161, 163, 166–68
Harman, Mary, 33
Harps, 76, 98, 101
Harry Potter series, 12, 119, 209
Harvey, 104
Hattridge, Anne, 156

Hedge leprechauns, 23, 39–40, 168–69, 194–95, 215
Hell, 6, 125
Hiram, King, 84
Hobgoblin, 35, 215. *See also* Goblins
Host, power of, 153
"Houses and Potatoes," 92–93
Hull, Josephine, 104
Human–fairy unions, 59
Hunchar, Zach, 210
Hygiene, 27–28, 48
Hynds, Anthony, 166–68

Iridich nan creag, 179
Irish Potato Famine, 91, 108, 200
An Isle Called Hirte, 33
Isle of Arran, 56, 69–70
Isle of Lewis, 38–39
Isle of Man, 83, 179
Ivarr II, King, 81–82

Jaffe, Tony, 202
James VI, King, 178
Jones, Mark, 209

Kavanagh, Herminie Templeton, 207
Kobolds, 168, 215
Koster, Henry, 207

La Fée de Lanascol, 73
La Légende de la Mort, 75
The Last Leprechauns of Ireland, 212
Laws, 141–46
Leaders, 138–40, 181
Leinster leprechauns, 108, 130, 133–36, 139–40
Leprechaun (comic book), 210–11
Leprechaun (film), 209
Leprechaun 2, 209–10
"The Leprechaun and His Hoard," 120–24

INDEX

Leprechaun Days, 203
Leprechaun hunts, 40, 212
Leprechaun series, 209–10
Leprechaun Whisperer, 212
Leprechaunism, 210
Leprechauns. *See also* Cluricauns;
   Fairies
   adaptability of, 194–97, 213
   in advertising, 201–5
   ancestors of, 84, 103, 161, 176–82, 189
   appearance of, 23–29, 66–68
   characteristics of, 5–6, 10–14, 67–68, 130–40, 168, 183–89, 197–200, 215–16
   clans of, 129–40
   cleanliness of, 27–28, 48
   clothing of, 24–27, 131, 136, 184, 199
   complexion of, 60, 67
   darker side of, 5, 16–17, 63–65, 125, 131–32, 161–68, 209
   description of, 5–6, 9–21, 23–29, 66–77, 215–16
   dwellings of, 5–6, 31–40, 91–94, 215
   finding, 31–46
   gender of, 55–77
   hair color of, 66–67
   hospitality from, 40–41
   as icons, 11, 15–17, 198–99
   laws of, 141–46
   lifespan of, 79–85
   lifestyles of, 10–11, 68–69, 127–216
   in modern world, 193–213
   nourishment for, 51–53
   occupations of, 87–96
   offerings for, 16–17, 52, 178–79, 187
   origins of, 6, 9–21
   overview of, 5–6, 9–21, 215–16
   in popular culture, 193–213
   pranks by, 105–7, 133–36, 155, 188, 197–98
   religion of, 147–59
   signs of, 17–21
   societies of, 129–40
   solitary nature of, 14–15, 33–34, 55, 67, 72–77, 83–84, 102–3, 109, 129, 179–81
   stereotypes of, 10, 179, 182, 198–200, 215
   temperament of, 10–14, 67–68, 130–40, 168, 183–89, 215–16
   terminology of, 11–13
The Leprechaun Companion, 55
Lewis chessmen, 38–39
Lianhan shee, 15
Lifespan, 79–85
Lifestyles, 10–11, 68–69, 127–216
Little people, 5–6, 9–23, 40–41, 169–82. *See also* Fairies;
   Leprechauns
"The Londonderry Air," 97
Lord's Prayer, 37, 164
The Luck of the Irish, 207
Lucky the Leprechaun, 202–3
Lughnasa, 107
Lughnasadh, 106–7

Macara Shee, 13–14, 37, 89, 103–4, 115
MacGregor, Alasdair Alpin, 32
MacKenzie, Roderick, 178
MacMurrough, King Dermot, 133
Macnamara, Niall, 55
MacNeill, Rúairí, 178–79
MacPhearson, Joseph, 156–57
MacQueen, Donald, 70
MacRúairí, Conchabhar Thadhg, 136
Malevolence, 154–58
May Day, 108

May Eve, 14, 103–5
McCormick, Robert, 169
McCurdy, Rose, 175
McInroy, Pat, 202
Mead, 135, 136, 181
Meadows, Jayne, 207
Meath leprechauns, 108, 130, 134–36, 140–42
Merriman, Brian, 137
Metalworkers, 94–96
Modern world, 193–213
Monasteries, 31–36, 133
Morrison, Alex, 175
Mounds, dwellers of, 5–6, 215. See also Fairy mounds
Mourne Observer, 40
Munro, Janet, 35, 207
Munster leprechauns, 102, 108, 130, 136–42, 183
Murphy, Minnie, 35
Murphy, Owney, 175
Music, 97–109, 112–14
Musicians, 97–109, 112–14, 137

New Statistical Account for Scotland, 70
Niall of the Nine Hostages, 82, 95
Norsemen, 59, 81, 180–82

O'Cahan, Rory Dall, 97
O'Carroll, Ferganainm, 138
Occupations
  bankers, 117–25
  blacksmiths, 94–96
  builders, 91–94
  entertainers, 111–16
  metalworkers, 94–96
  musicians, 97–109, 112–14, 137
  shoemakers, 13, 15, 26, 29, 47, 89–91, 197, 204
O'Coinn, Michaeleen, 130
O'Dea, Jimmy, 207

Odin the Wanderer, 83–84
O'Donovan, John, 190
O'Grady, Donagh, 64
O'Hagan, Priest, 148–52
O'Hare, P.J., 211
O'Hartigan, Dunlaing, 59
O'Kane, Teig, 163
"The Old Dudeen," 186
O'Malley, 98–101
O'Neill, Ferganainm, 138
Ordnance Survey, 156, 190
O'Reirdon, Michael, 81–82
Ormsby, Robert, 65
O'Sullivan, Sean, 77
Otherworld, 5–6, 100, 104
O'Tunney, Rúairí, 190–91
The Outer Hebrides and Their Legends, 71

Pagan gods, 147–56, 164, 191
Pagan sites, 36–38, 105, 149–51
Paradise, 65, 148–53
Peat, 45, 46
The Peat Fire's Flame, 32
Pechts, 11, 169–70
Phantoms, 154–55, 165. See also Ghosts
Poltergeists, 155
Pooka, 35, 67, 104, 105
Popular culture, 104, 193–213
Posti, Dylan, 210
Poteen, 16, 42–53, 103–4, 111–12, 142, 187–88
Power, Tyrone, 207
"Power over the Dead," 165–68
Pranks, 105–7, 133–36, 155, 188, 197–98
Prayer, 37, 164–65
"The Priest and the Leprechaun," 148–52
"Purse of the shilling," 17

INDEX

Rainbows, 118, 208
Rebels, 134
Religion, 147–59
Reproduction, 56–57
Rock-trolls, 215
Rowling, J.K., 12
Ruins, 31–36, 49, 72–75, 133, 143, 157, 190, 192
Rushy men, 46

Saint Brigid's Day, 105–6
Saint MacCuagh, 35–36
Saint Patrick, 124, 143
Saint Patrick's Day, 50, 106, 203, 205, 211
Saint Stephen's Day, 107
Saint Walpurga, 104
Seymour, St. John, 155, 158
Shamrocks, 38, 106, 205
Shape-shifters, 56, 69, 75, 104
Sheela-na-gigs, 189–92
Shillelagh, 199, 205, 206
Shoemakers, 13, 15, 26, 29, 47, 89–91, 197, 204
Sídhe, 5–6, 46, 60–64, 103
Snedeker, Alan, 203
Societies/clans, 129–40
Solomon, King, 84
Sports, 205–6
Sprites. *See also* Leprechauns
   characteristics of, 10–14, 67–68, 130–40
   description of, 23–29, 66–77
   finding, 31–46
   offerings for, 178–79, 187
   temperament of, 10–14, 67–68, 130–40
"Staff of Jesus," 143
Standing stones, 37–38, 149–51, 171, 177
Steele, Tommy, 208
Stevenson, Robert, 207

Stewart, Jimmy, 104
Stone, Mary, 170
Supernatural Highlands, 69
Superstitions of the Highlands and Islands of Scotland, 33
Swire, Otta, 71

Talla, 179
Technology, 193–98
Thompson, Frances, 69, 70
Tolcarne Troll, 83–85
Traps, 198
Tribunals, 142–46
Trolls, 83–85, 215
Tuatha dé Danann, 6, 17, 21, 56–57, 67–69, 91, 101

Uisnech, 108
Ulster leprechauns, 102, 108, 130–32, 135, 139–42
Urbanization, 193–98

Vanathee, 72–73
Vawnilds, John, 172
Viking ancestors, 180–82
Viking kings, 81–83

Walpurgis Night, 104
Warlock series, 211
Wee people, 5–6, 9–23, 40–41, 169–82. *See also* Fairies; Leprechauns
Witches, 19–20, 56, 66, 104, 107–8, 156, 177
Wizards, 56, 69, 180, 203
Woods, Kevin "McCoiltte," 211–12

Yeats, W.B., 13, 14, 129
Yule, 107

ABOUT THE AUTHOR

Bob Curran was born and raised in the Mourne Mountain region of County Down, Northern Ireland. Leaving school, he worked in a variety of jobs, including manual and clerical work, in the Civil Service, and as a journalist. While love of folklore and other cultures never left him, he left Northern Ireland for a time.

On his return, he went to university and then into teaching. He later returned to university to complete a PhD and lecture. He has written many books in various languages—Spanish, Korean, Chinese, Russian, French, and Polish, to name several. He has also produced a number of comics both in America and Eastern Europe, and has recently founded the Fool Moon imprint in both Europe and the US.

Although officially retired, he has served as an advisor to the Northern Ireland Assembly, and more recently has returned to university to head a major project on the Spanish Armada in Ireland. He currently lives on the Irish north coast with his wife and family.

THE LORE AND LEGENDS OF YOUR FAVORITE
MYTHICAL CREATURES!

PICK UP OR DOWNLOAD
YOUR COPIES TODAY!

adamsmedia
An Imprint of Simon & Schuster
A CBS COMPANY